T0247360

Lucida Intervalla

John Kinsella

LUCIDA INTERVALLA
A Novel

DALKEY ARCHIVE PRESS

Library of Congress Cataloging-in-Publication Data

Names: Kinsella, John, 1963- author.
Title: Lucida intervalla / John Kinsella.
Description: First Dalkey Archive edition. | McLean Il : Dalkey
Archive Press, 2018.
Identifiers: LCCN 2018026155 | ISBN 9781628972887 (pbk. : alk.
paper)
Classification: LCC PR9619.3.K55 L83 2018 | DDC 823/.914--dc23
LC record available at https://lccn.loc.gov/2018026155

www.dalkeyarchive.com
McLean, IL / Dublin

Printed on permanent/durable acid-free paper.

Acknowledgements

This novel has been composed across many years, and many texts by Søren Kierkegaard (and some texts relating to his life and works) have been read and distorted in the process of rethinking (especially the edition: Kierkegaard, S., & Capel, L. *The Concept of Irony: With Constant Reference to Socrates*, (Collins: London, 1966). The main source of Grimm's tales consulted and utilised in the creation of the 'Snow White' song text was Margaret Hunt's 1884 translation.

I wish to thank Alex Andriesse Shakespeare and Christopher DeVeau at Dalkey Archive for their care and consideration with this text, and Kate Pickard and Terri-Ann White at UWAP for the same. Also thanks to Curtin University where I am Professor of Literature and Environment, and to Nicholas Birns for his support and belief in this creation. Always thanks to my partner Tracy Ryan, and to the literatures and philosophies this work converses with. And special thanks to Lucida, who doesn't like me much and would disagree with most of what I have to say. She determines her own paths, many of which I find frightening.

'Outside Centralia, the world is amorphous. Only Perth and Copenhagen are real, even if the details of their existence are sketchy and, mostly, entirely absent.'

– Duke, as channelled by Lucida Intervalla

Lucida Replies to The Questions: When Did You First Become Interested in Art? And When Did You Become an Artist?

Dear Philomena,

Earlier than you might think, and later than you might think. I was ten. I had met all the requirements for art and craft in my early primary school years, and done adequately, but it hadn't really mattered to me. I thought of art as pictures, and pictures were about stories. It has been said that I have never *really* been an artist, and that I am little more than a documenter of other people's art. It's true I was never formally trained, but I might claim a second-to-none knowledge of the history of art. But when I was ten, instead of handing in my picture of a horse, I handed in a description of an imagined picture of a horse. And when that effort was chastised, I took a sheet of paper and soaked it with my school milk and told teacher it was a picture of a ghost. For that, I was given lunch-time detention and had to write a hundred times over in chalk on the blackboard: Spilling my milk on paper is not art. By the time I had finished the requirements of my punishment, I considered myself a true and committed artist. It has been my passion ever since.

Best wishes,

Lucida Intervalla, Centralia

Background

Søren Kierkegaard was born on the fifth of May, 1812, in Copenhagen under the sign of the butterfly. Infinite qualitative difference loomed large over the crib, and the smiling face of God flexed its antennae and declared itself only to be rebuffed by the baby with what we might now translate as, 'I know you are but a mobile, a piece of paper and cloth operating as a mind-opener, a visual amusement, even a distraction . . . you are not God but through you I might reach God, so there's nothing but passion in this. But I will hold back and say more later.' Immediately it was asked, making no connection with this event, who is the subject in this? But no slight was intended.

Confidence is a dodgy commodity. Petrarch imagined this to Laura on a cold morning when the bug wouldn't bite. It was the time to close the door on Latin once and for all. Little did he know that in 2020 it would come back with a vengeance, being enforced as the lingua franca of THE NEW WEST. And this is why I offer my declensions on a platter and leave myself open to the judgement of you, my readers. Houses. Chairs. Planes. Cars. And the memory of icebergs, mere slivers in polar waters. In a nutshell, I am *in form*: thanks!

Lucida Preliminaries Revamp

KIERKEGAARD WROTE HIS dissertation on irony. He wrote irony like law. In the modified distance between light on and light off, or absence of light altogether, we have this. And this. Test the waters. The stone echoes we cross by. Thus spake Lucida.

She continued: It was entitled, *The Concept of Irony: With Constant Reference to Socrates*.[1] I have a copy of an English translation of that work here now for The Boys to rework into digestible fragments for posting four times a day over the coming year. It makes for pretty Instagram pics.

In the intro to Kierkegaard's journal, the editor notes that it was written with 'some pathos.' Lucida has no choice but to upload it into her evolving character. It was, after all, pre-ordained. In its actuality was the true biography of the great artiste, Duke. And through Duke, the becoming of Lucida, who could only be far greater than what had come before. We read:

> And you, too, my *lucida intervalla* [bright intervals], I must bid farewell, and you, my thoughts, imprisoned in my head, I can no longer let you go strolling in the cool of the evening, but do not be discouraged, learn to know one another better, associate with one another, and I will no doubt be able to slip off occasionally and peek in on you – Au revoir!

---

1 Kierkegaard, S., & Capel, L. *The Concept of Irony: With Constant Reference to Socrates* (Collins: London, 1966). Also source of related quotes that follow.

S.K. (The Duke)
formerly Dr Exstatricus

And so, in looking back over a life of protest by default, Lucida found her *true* beginning. She said, Whenever I paste a piece of text from the web into a Word document it defaults into Lucida Bright. Into bright bright. It's a sign.

And in editing the sayings and anecdotes of Duke for public consumption, Lucida and The Boys bore the reality of Lucida following and erasing Duke's claim on *presence*. So when you read Duke, you read even more Lucida. We all interpolate, Lucida told The Boys, and Duke was, in a sense, always becoming me, too.

Utterances of Duke as Conserved and Presented by Lucida

IT IS IMPOSSIBLE to write a biography of the philosopher, the artist, or the artist's doppelgänger. What they are is unrecordable. It is not possible to describe a desert. In the end, we have to resort to the picturesque. The explorer's notebook, the artist's sketchbook, are, in the end, propaganda.

And as I only have a few days to type this out before retreating back to the desert, or into a forest that has become desert, back to proverbial *would*, I hope for bright interval, bright bright interval to get down. *Contraindication?*

A hypocrisy in light of damnation's follow-on. Probably. No, yes, entirely. I make no excuse. I request this record, if it is printed, be done on recycled paper. That, handed round in person, from protest to protester, it finds its way out into world outside usual structures of book-making, selling. Anyways, p(r) op-ups aside, what follows is honest accounting as far as I can recognise from life as protest against the mores of artworks. The grass has grown under my feet, on my back, and between my teeth. I have been fecund – a petri dish for creativity.

At times, I admit, I have been what the press malignly calls a professional protester, but as I earn no money [from it] and usually make do, earn my keep from the general pool, sup of the pool of food and shelter, or, moving between protests, take seasonal work, labouring with the fewest possible ironies. I reject epithet.

These 'confessions of . . .' are a record independent of drives and agendas of media, of serial protest across a period of twenty years – I am almost the link they have in common, outside a general political causation. But this is not my story and these are not my voices. This *fait accompli*. I won't explain more, just come for a wander through the/se life-story(ies) and see for yourself – first memory is of CLOUDS, of a page, a canvas, a clearing made with a bulldozer. Sublime. The cross as a plough, a plough's tine, a harrow. This is not really surprising as my mother uttered unto me from time she was pregnant with me, from the time she began staring at the she-clouds, from the time when I-she-conceived near the city steeples, or off the coast of my native Denmark, looking out into the deep Viking seas all lusty and pious.

My darling, my little darling, she would say, I watched horses become trees and trees become grandma and you and Papa loved me in the closet. And thus on heels I knitted a formula – little diagrams making narratives and beckoning towards clothes donation bins: he will stick his fist into a cop's face when the latter shone [shines] a torch down, peeking in. Part One dissertation I say, '. . . and it is therefore with profound irony that Aristophanes, in the scene where Strepsiades is supposed to be initiated into this wisdom, has Socrates invoke the clouds, the aeriform reflection of his own hollow interior.' That is I He-speaking, me, in my She portion, but I hand it over to you now, Duke – go forth and make artworks in the womb of the world and liberate me from your father. He speaks I for all of us. This little gathering, cluster of characters, artistes. We who tell you how the world is and will no longer be. *Now* says something to me about me and the state of my she-origins.

It also says that my lightly religious mother-to-be, who was outwardly happy to be *made love* to by her hosier-employer husband-to-be – that false grandfather of existentialism – must have in actual fact regretted consent and worshipping my cloudy consecration somewhat dissembled as moi (the foetus-to-be) continues, 'Clouds superbly characterise the utterly flabby thought process, continually fluctuating, devoid of footing and devoid of immanental laws of motion . . .' Fiercely overlooking her growing brood, Mother prepared us for future background checks, ensured we could quote appropriate texts, and vote to keep the borders secure. Delve deep, she'd say. As the shepherd (Father), delved deep on the grasslands as sheep ate the feet of God, and the horror of large, open spaces in such a small country impels a need to pass down via the DNA route a longing for said large open spaces. Embrace the contradictions, Duke-to-be. From small flocks of sheep to sheep stations Down Under! Follow the Southern Cross, my son.

In case you fear I am going to render my entire ironic life ironic, and, consequently, the causes I invoke as, by extension, laughable, I want to end that now-tone, as it never fixed things in my experience, and smiling compatriots on barricades can change a tone as quickly as acquiring it.

We all know a student joins company they protested against when it was what was expected of them. We've all been betrayed by the fellow who has an epiphany and warns the 'authority' for *our* own good. Seriously, my mother invoked *mea culpa* clouds around me all her life as my Mother, as I was child to her in her mothering. By the time I went on to learn the ways of me she was dead and buried and my father was trying to spark my inanimate body into a life of enterprise and profit.

But what do I know of that knowing of she? Nothing. I know forces of lightness are gathering like bleached horizon, that I dined with members of the British Nuclear forces, that bad reviews 'dismantling me' are coming. I dined early on out at Emu Plains and I dined on mushrooms and gravy and I witnessed the art of the clean-up and I came again to behold the legacy. I was forward-looking, sure, but more than that I shared their epiphany at the power of me in the face of the power of the Absolute. Time is neither here nor there.

Some others have got together and arranged assaults on my knowing and the despair I feel at the willingness to go the whole hog knows no bounds. They've recruited the young. They've recruited the novelists and songsters, they've recruited the well-schooled painters. They and I are below par. Have to admit. This scape I landsat. This gag I brace my arm against.

Don't think I don't remember. Who accounts for the hundred percent, who accounts for the brain blanks, lack of primogeniture. True, I she-filmed my own walk in her lost woods and came up pug-ugly and empty-handed out of Jutland. I mean, the Old Man retired at forty and with all that time on his hands had nothing better to do than pontificate. Myth-making paraphernalia, gate-keepers of the script, of the fonts of the future.

Knowing Lucida long before she appeared on the event horizon, long before she even *was* – it was foretold, her rising. Her wagon wheeling across the headlands, across the steppes, across deserts, treading down forests, dispersing the sheep. And her first True Love, Ben, would also be her true friend, and her slight of him is the extra wheel around which this tragedy turns.

Hello, Ben, I said, on her behalf. Knowing her becoming. Hello, be my friend old Ben-friend of my she-mum who is younger than me, who will be ETERNALLY young. My espalier to my vine. Ben said: don't get romantic on me, she counts little for you, she is mine though I know otherwise (the gall of it, laughed Lucida, letting it ride, wanting all for the record of truth). I rid(e) with Joo-an. I ride the metrics like a hayride.

My friends gather and make life so much harder. No names stick, and that makes it difficult. Awkward. But over a lifetime friends come & go, don't they? We hush Stelazine behind our backs. I inside my I-head, my character head, when I say what I see: fences brought down by storm trees, foxes feather at tails from mange, and roo shooters blooding genital ways. It's true, I tell you writing me. True as Indonesia = ash at the bottom of their craters. As if history is my fixation on smegma. Okay, hear me loud in cloud. Duke Kierkegaard, with home I dabbled and titillated roses, which laws Iggy's veins rise by, and track paramount audience feature. I was there, on bored, on the rise of televisual moment.

And so the Dr cut my foreskin and made culture of my body. This is a body moment in my book, a taking-stock of skin's distensions and folds, lack of tip. *I rit my tip off, I offed the bunny tail* and asbestos – raw, blue – sat on my bedhead. A childgrow in asbestos brackets, a box to breathe by and capture weathers:

those *whethers* and wethers in farm glow, a Christmas table I sat apart from, cracking crackers. And so I grew into being an agnostic Australian of rural extraction, when in fact I owed my heritage to the Lutheran and kicking against the pricks, ended up shipping out on a four-masted schooner. Family Bible inscribed to belong to me but not mothers'. Gentry oscillation of family rejoinders. I sat on the tractor and ploughed Home, boy, home.

So, I'll tell you, I see: clay dirt clagging the discs, a runnel of super and pickled grain, an early emergent weed knockdown, feed potential as exponential as the John Deere. I DON'T HEAR TOO WELL WITH THE EAR-PLUGS JAMMED IN SO TIGHT THOUGH ALL VIBRATIONS COLLECT FOR LATER ANALYSIS STRICTLY IN A STRICT SENSE I HEAR WELL AFTER THE SOUND HAS PARSED STRICTLY SPEAKING I HEAR YOU THROUGH YOUR HEARING ME YOU SEE I PLAYED GUITAR IN FRONT OF THE TV AND THAT WAS MY COMPANY; what plea is had out-side grand hotel grand station grand plan I unfold to detriment neighbours and indeed myself as I tell tales on myself to spite myself as lyrical as all get up in the strips of bark shed because it's time of year because trees will shed before growing rough fireproof bark back because they survive need of seething climate seething responsibility to grow up and out and make a mess of skyline we build with furrows and windrows – I plant and grow and cut and plant and grow and cut; so what irony is crime per se is crime bona fide as the quid pro quo of my narrowness to fill silos and collect the wheat cheque.

I will move on, telling minstrel-like of *Duke Kierkegaard's* telling of myself as denial is sacred chow is gargoyles and gorgons rising up out of the sea bed reinvested carbon dioxide beneath the Barrow Island Arc beneath fox-free cat-free marsupial wonderland so think about that, those splin-ters and hanks of true cross and where I was in the holy lands reading *Clarel* alone with the secrets of text as projects (*the*) close to my heart as cedars of Lebanon, great karris of the Porongurups just near Devil's Slide at 670 metres; and this summit, so open about me, upon which I write honestly, you who write and read only in rooms, on subways in libraries in cities, under a shady tree: no such, no such, no such!

And thus spake Lucida[2], speaking Duke's words and writing his writing, and letting her flow flow freely and he, being he, took up the mantra and rolled with her. Gloriously their social conditioning wed and blossomed and made a mountain of molehills, and echidnas turned them over for termites. Lucida, standing on Mount Victoria looking out onto the neighbouring mountain where Duke had once squatted (the concrete house that perches there, defying the odds and weight of antennae), said we sign so many treaties, and we rescue what we can from the Opium Wars, and the grain traders of Australia drink a toast to weapons and wheat and the cultural slippage of the me in the world, of the us and them and the you in freewill. Lucida loved Duke, and always would, but her brief time with him weighed heavily and a price had to be paid. And the price, always, is fame. And this, she would say with her last breath, is all of my moments crammed into this, right now, and I've almost enough breath left for Duke too, that old rogue.

2 A trick, a ploy – it's her modus operandi, be forewarned . . . She's sucking you in, playing voices like dress-up with paper dolls she didn't have and would have burnt if she had.

Pisstake

SERIOUSLY, DO YOU think I value myself beyond the arc of the diver. It's so sincere, observing and *capturing* – this art-making. Caught in your parody, I manifesto my way to liberty. Contemplate the flight, the shift away. A death, and you only twenty-one. A severance pay. Glib as the sincerity of the critic stumped, floored and flabbergasted (me). A slow but steady rain that washes away the topsoil nonetheless. Seriously, where do you expect me to look, déshabillé, stockings on my hairy legs ransacked and gloating. Those golden knickers. That pink floppy hat. You leave yourself open, you do, open to a good bashing. Not a sound thrashing – that dilutes the crime (how perverse is that?!). I mean, what's left of the Brandenburg Concertos once you take out the false notes of the violin: the soothing in the face of violence, Bale's taking up the sword for the New Jerusalem. It's all violence really, and thus the cult of death. Though there, mostly, maybe, it's the end of violence being worshipped. The means to an end. See, the sincerity shines through the pisstake, the truth in the absurdity. It stumps them all. She was his (the grandfather of existentialism!) second wife, back in Copenhagen where he'd gone to live with Uncle after the sheep had bolted. But I am crossing life stories. But then again, how are they to be separated? You can't protest bits of us being in all of us as we're parts of the same. Surely?

What Makes You So Special, Lucida?

DURING RECESS AND lunch, Lucida always sits on her own. She doesn't participate in group activities if she can avoid them. She is sullen and occasionally rude. *She is extremely intelligent but underachieves.*

Lucida liked that part of her Year 8 final report and cut it out and stuck it above her bed. It is better than a prayer, she said.

Year 9 became in the same way. Different teacher same old same old. Lucida, you should mix more. Lucida, don't you have any friends? Lucida, you have a morbid fascination for dissection – it's just science, nothing more nothing less. It could be so much more, insists Lucida.

And the days grind on and she smokes in front of the change rooms, and not behind. There are other 'different' girls behind the change rooms. She is suspended. She returns. The teacher says, Make an effort to be liked, Lucida! You make life hard on yourself. Lucida says, Life is not a popularity contest. I am no bimbo on Miss World. That's very precocious of you, Lucida. How so? You shouldn't talk like that, young miss. Why not? And what makes you think you're so special, Lucida? I won't be making any exceptions for you – if I did, it would be letting you down. You *want* to turn into a nice person, Lucida, and it's my responsibility to help you on your way, and I take that responsibility seriously. Seriously? asked Lucida.

In social studies students were asked to describe their ethnicity and cultural heritage. Why bother? asked Lucida, Take a look around you – all good Anglo-Celtic stock and one girl from

Goa. I've just done the survey *for you*. That's rude to highlight one student, Lucida. That's what you're doing. No, Lucida, we're celebrating difference. Difference? Here, in this school with its thousands of dollars' fees and vetted intake and old white families of Perth foundations? Who are you kidding. Lucida added that she herself had no ethnicity and no culture and no school. She was suspended a second time. They allowed her back when she (erroneously) claimed she was born in Jutland, a suburb of Bunbury.

Lucida was expelled when she painted a self-portrait in menstrual blood. She was sent to a 'child' psychiatrist but only attended one session. He told her guardians that he couldn't help her. She was in total control.

*

Lucida wanted to play the guitar but didn't want to waste time learning. She strummed a few chords and decided she would talk to guitarists about what they did and then retell it in her own words.

*

On the cover of *Guitar World*, Keith Richards was leaning against Duke with his arm hooked up over his shoulder. Duke is my main man, Keith was quoted as saying. Inside, an interview by Duke with Keith Richards that talked about 'off-beat' things (favourite colour, least liked food, best teacher, worst teacher). Lucida had an epiphany.

*

As a very small girl, Lucida had eaten a roll of blue streamer crepe. It had dyed her mouth blue, and made her vomit blue tapeworms. She didn't tell anyone but snuck past the long wooden plant holder that divided the front door of the house off from the loungeroom, then down the corridor where she turned left and on into the master bedroom. She closed the door and looked in the mirror, which stretched the full length

of the door and made her longer than she was. Blue vomit and
partially dissolved crepe covered her mouth and white pinafore.
She was a sight, as adults would say. Surely. She laughed and
it was a hideous laugh, but she was neither possessed nor evil
so we can't really say that, can we. But we can say, by any nor-
mal standards of aesthetics, that the expulsion of the crepe had
not made her pretty, prettier, or even as pretty (or not) as she'd
been before. Lucida smeared some of the bile-blue goop on the
mirror, and painted around the outline of her reflection. Above
her illustration, in a tilted gloriole, she formed her name which
was the first word she ever wrote, this being her first occasion of
writing. She wrote it perfectly, in more or less Gothic lettering.
Blue Gothic. She loved the effect. She extended the halo so it
became a mandorla and she stepped into the mirror and became
her desecrated reflection. She liked it a lot better than Sunday
School which she was too young to attend, really, but was made
to attend and colour in the pictures of Jesus with the disciples
and there was a boat and a lake and she kept going outside the
lines and the teacher would say, Stay inside the lines, Lucida.
Our Lord wasn't spiky like that. Lucida instinctively knew the
word 'radiant' though she didn't use it because she knew it would
serve her ill. And stepping back out of her reflection she pulled
off her pinafore and rubbed at the mirror to remove the evidence
of where she had been and how she had got there. The smears
blurred her out of the picture and she couldn't think of any way
the adults would know she'd been there. I am no longer in the
mirror, she thought. She took her pinny to the sandpit and buried it. And then she heard her name being called from the studio
at the back of the garden where the adults had been working,
absorbed in their own creativity. She bolted inside and to the
bathroom and washed and tried to find a clean pinny before
dark shadows loomed through the house and punished her for
nothing, nothing at all.

*

There was a friend. It was a girl. She was six and Lucida was
six. There was Ben, later, of course. But before Ben there was

another friend. That friend only stayed a friend for a week. It was a holiday in a caravan park friendship. Somewhere near the sea, but a bit back. You had to walk to the sea where you couldn't swim because of clots of seaweed, and cobblers, and stingers and sharks. The weed stank to high heaven. Phew!

The friend's name was Rhea. They both had buckets and spades and dug in the small patches of damp sand that weren't covered in weed. They carved cuttlefish with driftwood. They laughed themselves silly. They played tricks on people in the toilets. They threw stones and sometimes shells if they could find them. They'd cart them back to the park in their buckets and hurl them onto the roofs of caravans.

Lucida's caravan was very large and grand and Rhea's was small and sad. There was a great storm that came up out of nowhere and Rhea's caravan was blown over and Rhea went away in the old car that had towed the caravan but the caravan was left broken on its side and all Rhea's life was spilled out and scattered by the storm and trodden down into the mud. Lucida wrote many words on the broken caravan walls – scratched with shell or stone into the paint. She wrote SHIT and LOVE and HATE and FOREVER and lovehearts. No one told her off, which surprised her.

The Tale of Ben

BEN WAS NO bunny. Ben loved Lucida. They made a swell couple. A grand couple. They felt strongly about issues, even if their friends said they were 'low-level thinkers.' Their friends were all graduates who felt they would make a contribution to the world. As philosophers and spiritual beings and consumers. Ben said to Lucida, Let's join the cause. Lucida didn't need to ask which cause, she knew. She and Ben had tuned in to each other. They simultaneously noticed that the city lights shimmering on the black river were like the flowers of mistletoe feeding off acacia acuminata, they were attuned enough to the South Perth fore-shore to step over the used syringes, to catch a Frisbee without landing in dog shit. Together, they compiled the story of the city – a cento. They took all the utterances of everyone and everything they could find and pasted them together. They didn't declare their sources. They didn't cite. We will be anathema, they giggled, pawing each other in the halflight of the Zoo, walking home, walking the long way home, suburbs away. They just liked to hang out in rich areas – didn't mean they lived there. Whenever they spoke they said, Come off it, they're not your own words, you can't use them, they're copyright. Falling down laughing, they both shat themselves to little bits. They loved each other's stench. Their fall would be public and gratuitous – the patent holders of words they spewed forth would show no mercy, and gained much attention, feeling that they were arbiters of the *major*. In the end, the king prosecutor said, They were always just *minor* and no skilled crafts . . . men – people – at all.

18

Roger Dodger

SINCERITY IS A bugger. Plato, being Socrates's gimp, or vice versa, is a troglodyte. I wouldn't believe him who left and came back with great claims either! Bitten by a rat, the braggart couldn't stop the spread of bugs in his own head. Saw shadows in broad daylight. We called him Roger Dodger but we were never there, never part of it. We are surface dwellers, purely and utterly. He was . . . he is . . . a self-indulgent entity. Rodger Dodger was Lucida's nickname for her male alter ego but she made me swear never to mention it. She herself said, having told me, she would never mention or think of it again. She has that capacity.

Irony, irony, irony . . .

Cloud costumes. Basket on a rope and the sun. Award us the prize. Hoodwink, fraudulence: iconoclasts or just exploiters, either way, we deserve our say and to be rewarded by those of you who hate us. I've always hidden behind plurals. Take this narrative, all these things happening to & fro, all these knife edges, all these immoral behind-the-scene indulgences, all these things you simply can't believe would or might or could be true. What do we want of you? From you? My name isn't William James Hickie, however far back I appeared (beforehand). Aristophanes is original in the original. Always bastardised, what philosopher is worth his salinity if not a reader of originals, especially in that era. Especially when under scrutiny. Examination. Let's read Mr Hickie's take on *Clouds*:

> Phidippides (talking in his sleep). 'You are acting unfairly, Philo! Drive on your own course.'

Or further on, as if his or our or your life depended on it (and admittedly it's just a random grab, and who cares what it actually says in translation or original? Hey, hey . . . I ask you! glory of Athens, glory of Western absurdity, the mirror we hold to our own cultural vanity, the splendor of laughter at the expense of?):

> 'Unj. And then she went off and left him; for he was not lustful, nor an agreeable bedfellow to spend the night with. Now a woman delights in being wantonly treated.

But you are an old dotard. For (to Phidippides) consider,
O youth, all that attaches to modesty, and of how many
pleasures you are about to be deprived – of women, of
games at cottabus, of dainties, of drinking-bouts, of giggling. And yet, what is life worth to you if you be deprived
of these enjoyments? Well, I will pass from thence to the
necessities of our nature. You have gone astray, you have
fallen in love, you have been guilty of some adultery, and
then have been caught. You are undone, for you are unable
to speak. But if you associate with me, indulge your incli-
nation, dance, laugh, and think nothing disgraceful. For
if you should happen to be detected as an adulterer, you
will make this reply to him, "that you have done him no
injury": and then refer him to Jupiter, how even he is
overcome by love and women. And yet, how could you,
who are a mortal, have greater power than a god?'[3]

Postscript: This is true – he actually said to me after a few too
many: 'Irony made me attractive to women, it made me a powerful person.' He said *person*. That's what gnawed at me. Really.
I listened to Pink Floyd's *Atom Heart Mother* through five times
in a row in the aftermath. I said to them, clearly, if you let the
temperature rise much further it'll all be kindling. Your paintings
will be burnt offerings: lushness, a speculative fiction. I said that
on my way to fame, on my way to pulling down an icon and
using it as a retread on the information superhighway. I can
afford to show my age. I am, definitively, ageless.

---

3 http://www.perseus.tufts.edu/hopper/text?doc=Perseus:abo.
tlg,00019,003:1068

Lucida's First Encounter with the Idea of Duke and Her Realisation She's Been Becoming Youth Since (At Least) Conception: Channelings

A POSTCARD FROM Denmark on a table. She climbs onto a chair and teeters, sees the postcard and grabs at it, falling. What are you doing, Lucida? Someone rushes over and picks her up and brushes her off and says, No broken bones, missy. What were you after? And then someone is handing her a postcard and saying, This is from Denmark. That's where your Uncle lives, all the way up in Europe. See the flag. And in each section of the flag is a picture of an attraction in the capital city, Copenhagen. And see that statue, Lucida? That naked man? Now at your age you don't want to get the wrong idea of what a naked man looks like – this one is all grim and yucky and distorted because it's *art*. It's by an artist called Duke and he comes to Australia a lot and now he's somewhere out in Centralia searching for what he calls the 'ineffable.' And then the adult was laughing at Lucida, and Lucida felt her face burn up and she bit the hand that fed her and the card fell to the ground with a yawp!

Boosterism

IF ENOUGH TIME passes between drafts and for the life of you you can't pick up the threads, newness blossoms. And, oh, how we need newness. In the lust for the tale, the craving for narrative, we scour the text for the folktale it is inevitably based on. Identity death-wish. Those caps popping at the highest part of the canopy, a rain of stamens. I read a tale in a book given to me by an adult. There was a king and his daughter who loved a golden bird. The golden bird sang to her on her balcony, luring her to the edge. The girl – princess – reached out only to fall as the bird flew laughingly away. Twisted and fatally wounded on the ground, an ugly rooster she'd spent many afternoons tormenting, saying, Crow, you old bastard! pecked at her wounds and turned her into a beautiful hen. He then had his way with her and the king, coming out, laughed to see such fun and said, Glad my daughter isn't around to see this . . . She has campaigned for the preservation of the rare and almost extinct Noisy Scrub Bird . . . She was an artist of the red list . . . She was the vision of futures past . . . She was the future of animal and plant kingdoms. 'Las, the Old Man's boosterism was sniggered at by princes in surrounding kingdoms who, nonetheless, thought the princess a bit of a stunner with a good dowry package to back it up. On the offer of her hand if they could find her – no one had any idea what had happened – all of them, all the eligibles,

tried their hand at tracking her down. All were deft hands with
a chainsaw. But none of them grew old searching – they gave it
their best, and moved on when it became obvious there was no
hope. I saw all this come to pass hitch-hiking Down South with
Ben. Ben and I conversed. I foretold my meeting with Duke.
It was just around the corner. Ben said, You speak and Duke's
words pour out of your mouth. And I yelled back in his face,
No more nookies for a month!

Taking a Peak

THE HIGHEST PEAK is the peak of guilt. But I – He/We – have double vision. We suffer. I can imitate anyone's accent, idiom, inflection. He can imitate their imitations. He can be incredibly silly. The word *silly* makes him laugh. English's

best onomatopoeia, he says. Alone and pondering the debasement through impersonal presentation, the act of performing sex for public consumption, he explored MILF sites for signs of self-irony. Age appropriate. Some guilt, but

not a lot. Most was at the expense of the older women featured in the photos and clips. Being amateur sites, one imagines these images were posted with acquiescence and even a sense of vanity with the knowledge a caption a titling of

the 'scene' would likely be derogatory. He wondered, taking a peek, if he was colluding with the abusers, those profiting in some way or another out of these sites. Or maybe they were collectives, a sharing of profits and sensuality, a site of

sheer enjoyment, no-holds-barred, a release. But he couldn't believe it and struggled with the stimulation he knew he should have. As Catweazle says, Nothing works. He – I – am a Danish Australian. I am forcing myself to write

in English, which I have spoken since I was a child, but I think

Danish has shipbuilding nuances that English can't go near.
Australian Danish. The Opera House. I – He – wondered if
that lifted him over the peak of guilt, if it made

him a better man for letting his doubts override his sensory soft-
ware, making the hardware irrelevant? Am I in this, in all of this,
too concerned with self, too preoccupied with my constituent
parts. Johannes Climacus reading his own

reports. I studied Latin at my school, and German. But they
didn't possess me – I climbed their peaks and saw the flatlands
of Denmark. I would call myself a Christian, but I spent all my
father's money on women and drugs. But that was

early on. Does it matter that this act of viewing takes place in
Copenhagen or in Mount Magnet, in a mining donga, with
other fellas close by, separated by a thin membrane of wall? Does
it matter that I actually read (each night) from the Bible

I lifted from the motel on the way up here, that I believe in
Christ and the resurrection, that I am an operator who wants to
become part of the inner-circle of management, to talk movies
and maybe even theatre with them? This drab

quotidian, this extraction of the greed-inducing metal, this 'how
I live' my life I struggle with alone. I had a wife. We left each
other. We were readers. I read what they call popular philosophy,
she read Hegel. My self, my universal self.

What else can I be but be preoccupied with the peaks. The
looks of grimacing ecstasy on the faces of the participants – the
women. I don't believe it and that means something has gone.
Sometimes you have to believe – agency, joy,

Divine Governance.

Lucida's Pinkie

SHE'D HAD MANY white and brown mice, but this one was pink! And it was lost and then in her bed and she was calling out, Pinkie has come back, but no one was going to get out of bed to see what had disturbed her – it was such a cold night.

Lucida had been dreaming of her lost mouse. It came from the shop with puppies in the window nipping each other and rolling in shredded newspaper. The shop smelt of piss and birdseed and there were many goldfish swimming and entangling in long thin tanks with lines of bubbles trying to reach the top from shipwrecks at the bottom of the deep deep deep. And there were mouse's houses with lots of pink and blue mice and she asked for a pink one and took it home in a cardboard box with airholes.

Not another mouse, Lucida! You've so many already and they keep on having more and more babies.

I keep their house clean and they always have water and food.

It was true. Lucida cared for her mice. She preferred her mice to people. She watched them go round and round on the wheel, and nibble the end of the water bottle. She carried them in her pockets and didn't mind their little poops sticking to her clothes.

But her favourite ever was Pinkie who grew into a big mouse, steadily becoming less and less pink – a boar who was always on top of the female mice and had made litter after litter. He had also eaten some of the newborns which she loved to watch all curled up in their finely woven paper nest, a film of skin over their eyes, suckling greedily at their mother. But Pinkie had eaten some and with blood on his *herbivore* mouth, he was a frightening sight and this clashing image ate into Lucida's brain. She told an adult and the adult said, Well, we can hit Pinkie on the head with a hammer. And Lucida rushed out and down to the shed and lifted Pinkie out by the tail and whispered in his ear, Go now Pinkie, go and hide. They're coming for you with a hammer. And thus Pinkie went into the wild open world with his ears sharp and blood on his snout. Across the shed floor and to an opening where boards didn't quite meet flush and into the walls then out into the long grass behind the shed. He was gone.

Lucida could not cope without Pinkie. She neglected her other mice and she gave another girl at school so many Chinese burns that the girl's mother wrote a note to the school and Lucida was taken up to the headmaster's office for a warning. We don't give little girls the sixes, said the headmaster. Though for you we might make an exception if you keep bullying other students. Fire with fire is my motto, he said as his face twitched and his colour changed and he rubbed just above his left knee.

But Pinkie had returned. Three weeks later and Lucida was dreaming of him and then she felt something warm at her feet and she woke as something ran up her leg and under her night-gown and up over her chest and poked its nose out from the collar and sniffed her chin. She gently lifted her hand and wrapped her fingers around the giant mouse, and lifted him close to the moonlight coming through the sleepout window, and hoisted herself up. Pinkie has come back! But it was cold and no one heard or listened if they did hear and she slunk back down and curled around her mouse and whispered, giggling, Sorry, Pinkie, I almost gave up on you. Good thing *they* are too stupid to take any notice, all curled up in their warm beds while you've been out in the cold. I'll make you a new secret house and we can see each other all the time.

And so, next morning, which was a Sunday, with Pinkie in her ballerina jewel box, Lucida dressed in her best clothes – a cheongsam given to her by a distant family member who had come back from years living in Singapore – and snuck out the back and over the webfrosted buffalo grass and down to the shed where she introduced Pinkie to his friends and family and let him have his way with some of the females while she deftly and quickly made a new home in which he would live secretly. But going back to the mouse house to retrieve Pinkie, she noticed blood on his mouth and realised he'd been at the litter of another couple and she said, Pinkie, you are simply incorrigible. She repeated *incorrigible* because it's what she was so often called. Now, into your new home. Here's some paper and water and food. We'll get you your own wheel. And she hid the new home behind a stack of old canvases that had never been painted. Someone had been a painter – one of the adults – but she didn't know which one and had never asked. Now, Pinkie, I will see you later. I will have to go to church soon. They will come down here looking for me and say, Lucida, get out of that dress and go and get some of your church-going clothes on. And I will eat porridge. But when I get back home I'll come straight down and say hello and some nights I will sneak you inside so that you can sleep in my bed again, just like you did last night. I am so glad we've found each other again, Pinkie, though I guess you really found me. You are a very clever mouse. A very clever and cuddly and big and dangerous mouse. It's just like the teacher says to me, Pinkie . . . she says, Lucida, there's nothing simple about you. Still waters run deep. We've got our place in the world, too, Pinkie, and no one is going to tell us otherwise. We've got to look out for each other. I will think of you when I am at church. You will be in my prayers.

Translation and the Drag of Being Duke

I AM SO tired of translation. Tired. Of being translated so they can get what I am on about. Translating to make ends meet. An end to translation. True, tried, and tested. The phrase book is the end of language. Google Translate is, worryingly, improving. The ironing-out. Articles abound, or drop out completely. Singing along with a rufous whistler the bright spark got the notion he could speak bird in all its languages. He chirruped and tweeted around the neighbourhood, and look now where it's got him.

Right, a redemption story. Translated out of, say, the South of France for a middle-class festival-going Australian audience. A books audience. There is always another life elsewhere, if you're willing to take the plunge. What was it Pedrillo tried to foist on us (lapped up by some) in *The Abduction from the Seraglio*? Yes, that's it: 'The worst slavery is liberated by joviality and booze.' The analogy is a case of mixed metaphors, but retaining anonymity is important to my *practice*.

Whispers, whispers. Still, intended to be overheard. Dramatic irony is the mainstay of this company. So, I am translating Pitt Morison's *Foundation of Perth* painted on its centenary in 1929 into binary. A lot of 0s and a bunch of 1s. Mrs Helena Dance is brightly vocal, swinging the axe. As I used to sit in the Perth Art Gallery as a young fella and teethe on it. Advertisement (G. Shenton, & Co. Chemists and Druggists, General Dealers, Agents, &c. – Perth, July 8th, 1840): 'Linen and cotton ticking, glazed muslins, brown and dark green merinos, bleached and unbleached calicos . . . deletion, acquisition, dispossession . . .

scotch plaids, dimities, duck, canvas . . . black swans, paperbarks, songlines . . . collars and caps, edgings, bobbin lace . . . cultural displacement from where penetration hasn't yet taken place . . . the mélange of anachronisms, the Cottesloe and Peppy Grove home of miners, politicians and entrepreneurs . . . unexploded ordnance (WWI grenade) hauled in off Applecross Jetty where I translated you all as a kid with a dragster bike, roaming . . . ledgers, journals, and memorandum books, foolscap and bath post paper, &c. &c.'

The fact that he didn't notice 'up-close' details was surely not a reflection *on* his intelligence, on his capacity to be receptive to his surroundings? There he was, about to walk off the wharf and up the gangplank onto the deck of an American guided-missile destroyer. What's more, he was in the company of a warrant officer (first class?) who was a good fifteen years older than his fifteen years (total). The decks were shiny grey (or 'gray'), as were the turrets. The doors were watertight. The officer's shoes were shiny. All the sailors' shoes were shiny. The missiles sparkled. Translating this into Bengali nothing was lost, I lost none of it, it was an exact, precise and perfectly correct translation. It was both literal and figurative, did not rely on dynamic equivalence though you could construe elements of this pertaining to one cultural experience but not the other, though working so well as a comparative model that who could tell the difference?

And to be frank about it, Holst's 'Mars: Bringer of War' is repulsive in its clarity and simplicity. Mind you, there's nothing subtle about its inspiration. Its grossness doesn't mean it should be deleted. And thus I began my speech against censorship, the audience shocked at the mere thought Holst's work would ever even be in the ambit of a discussion about *suppression*.

Søren Kierkegaard was born on the fifth of May, 1812 in Copenhagen under the sign of the butterfly.

Asbestos Roses

AROUND THE ROSE beds the dirt was really the black sand of the coastal plain. It needed covering over, to give body to the walkways between the rose beds, dark and thick with mulch. Foundation for the gravel to be spread over. Those red roses, so deeply coloured. Crimson, in fact. Dozens of asbestos sheets left over from building . . . here and there. And teenagers gathered together for the bust-up: sheet on sheet smashed and trampled and embedded into the coastal plain sand. Fibres dressing cuffs and boots and making flurries from the ground up up up. And then the gravel poured from barrows to tamp it all down.

And thus past the roses down under the gables of the arched house, past the kookaburra leadlight porthole, bay window, red and white camellias, popping fuchsias, across the cemented courtyard and down through the shadehouse dripping with staghorns and orchids, across the gravelled area encircling the Great Mulberry Tree to the incinerator where all things burn, including tyres and cuttings from grapevines holding trellis on trellis together. This journey is more than an expedition, it is a feat of the imagination. You could stop by the concrete troughs where horse manure festers under tin sheets, redbacks clinging to shadows, their globular egg-sacs ready to set their grip on territory. You might pick almonds and find grubs in the heart of the seeds, a pinpoint entry or exit in the nutshell, the smooth tearing of the tear of the nut to find the threaded waste of occupation. 'Great art is always delicate.' Ruskin? Yes, I believe so. Off the top of my head, Dirty paper makes art delicate. Delicatessen of

32

scrawl. Or sprawl? You've caught me on the hop. Distracted by catechism, which is skewiff to doctrine. Having fallen from the one true. Truth – the sign lasted decades. I flourished on *low art*. There's an asbestos garage with an old Premier Holden automatic therein, its tyres painted with white circles – white walls. But the car has been backed out of the garage and an elderly man, an artist, is painting a sign (he is a signwriter by trade) with words and a flourish of Western Australian wildflowers in each corner. They are his appeasement of his art, a reconciliation of responsibility and desire. As he leans on his rest, looking intently through the necessary points of his bifocals, he is humming a tune. Gladys Moncrieff. And he is thinking of his mother, his much-loved mother, playing the piano at the Grand in Perth, accompanying the movies. Silent movies. He believes he doesn't know. He says to himself, to us all, 'I don't know, and nor do you . . . sister, brother . . .' During the Bodyline series he managed to get the signatures of all players on both sides. He got Bradman's signature three times over the decades. And once, only once, as a young man, Charles Kingsford Smith. He thought of this, or rather he thought of thinking of this fact when, watched over by Red Guards, he and his wife examined the 'perfect' remains of Lenin in his mausoleum in Red Square, Moscow. When was that . . . ? Late '60s? 1970. What precisely *was* the Cold War?

A lemon falls from the lemon tree – it's ripe, but not overripe – and leaves flutter from tall trees onto the garage roof. He laughs to himself. One tramp seeing another tramp with one shoe on and the other foot bare, asks his comrade, 'Did you lose a shoe, mate?' and the semi-shod tramp replies, 'No, mate, found one!' I mean, you've gotta laugh and keep a steady hand at the same time. Sign done and dusted.

ENTRY FEES: Adults $1.50
               Children 20c
               Concessions (show card) 50c

What Would I Know About It? Ben Speaks Out

TELL ME ALL about it, I am all ears . . . You're *proving* human-induced climate change is an academic ruse? Sorry, an 'extreme green' ruse? Green should be capitalised. Now, I'll tell you about something I saw the other day – a sticker (next to a fish) in the back of a 'people-mover' van as we headed down the Scarp past Red Hill waste disposal area . . . it said, 'Beat the Extreme Greens' and had a picture of a tree with a red cross through it. So . . . chop down trees as a political act of . . . control? A preventative action? Some teachers take schoolkids on tours of Red Hill . . . asbestos disposal, highly toxic substances . . . the city's garbage. Not far from the sacred granite rocks known as 'The Owl.' So, tell me more about rising temperatures? Oh, they're not? Okay. I'm interested. You were saying about the Ice Age and 'twas ever thus . . . ?

'Infinite Absolute Negativity' – Ben, Influenced by Lucida and the Idea of Duke, Hangs Out with an Erstwhile Mate, Benji

So you think irony fails to progress the human condition?

Ben asked this through pursed lips, a stream of smoke escaping as he did so, then a hacking cough collapsing into a snigger as he passed Benji the bong. I've just gotta get this bibliography sorted and a few footnotes in and it will go off to the binders. Scholarship is coming to an end anyway so I mean I might as well submit. I know it's a load of bullshit and I've got no respect for titles . . . can you imagine going around calling myself Dr?

Nah, mate, I can't. You'd be a real wanker if you did that. You'd be a little bitch, you would!

Yeah, I'll just get the bit of paper and burn it. Just bought time to do my art, really.

Yeah (snigger) and buy heaps of good hydro and share it with ya real mates!

Nothin' truer, buddy, *nothin'* truer. Feel like a game? I'm pumped, I reckon I'll have you this time, you're just another False Master.

Ya reckon . . . in ya dreams, mate, in ya dreams!

And then one of them mounts the other, fully clothed, and starts dry humping. Hump hump hump. Come on, mate, enough. Stop! Get off me ya bastard. It's not funny, you're fucking hurting me! And then there's a flash a slash and someone is dying. It's that simple. And the inadequacy of language deployment, the lack of grit and brand names, the peculiarities of a piece of carpet viewed up close by the victim in the moments before death, are lacking. Where is the flourish, where is the verve, where is the creative research?

Protesting the Industrialisation of Love: Ben at a Loose End While Lucida Pursues Her Dream

Lost in the moment, Ben dragged himself free by switching the reception to Iggy Pop's 'I'm Bored.' *Chairman of the Bored.* And then he began to unpick the narrative of his personal deception – or, to clarify, his deceiving of himself. The humidity had made the York gum foliage heavy and more than one tree in his remit lost limbs – torn away from the body by the stress of the weight they bore. Back in the country. He returned to the wheatbelt when depressed. Lucida had lost interest in him again. Again. He was, he knew, her gimp. Being gimp was part of it, or maybe it was all of it. The loss, the reasoning through. A case of loss aversion – rather than hope for gain, he wished desperately to avoid loss. Loss was more than a rug from out under his feet, it was totality. A synonym for death. *Case theorem.*

Ben checked his holdings and the kingdom he laid claim to. All those rates-payers, all those embodiments of love (towards him, his shining light). The efficient and profitable manufacture of love is always considered a desirable risk by the NSA and its Australian cousins. The in-built flaw is repulsion, the popular rejection of FREAKS. Sidewalks. Kerbs. Pavements. Footpaths. Carnivale. All raw ingredients. One day, he told himself, It will be left to me to write the biography of Duke. Lucida can never play second fiddle. Never. I dance to the piper. Always been the way.

Lucida Consigns One Dream to the Trash

LUCIDA THOUGHT ABOUT letting Ben know she was back in town but decided against it. She'd seen things few others had ever seen. She'd sat at the steps of the Danish People's Church, she'd robbed Peter to pay Paul, she'd uncovered the treachery of being bonded to family. Amazing what a little DNA testing can do, she told thin air. There's no way I'm acting as a vector for that kind of family wealth. So much for sacrifice. What am I left with, wondering? This exceptional skill set left bereft. My universal translator body placed on the pyre of self. And so, signing the register, and consulting with the undertaker, and wrestling over my visa, and lamenting the passing of my Europass, I see in reverse writing on every situation: *Infandum me jubes Lucida renovare dolorem.* And so I inscribed my *Let's Go.* And so I calibrated my vocation.

Lucida Scores the Assignment: Interviewing Duke

As THE FRONT approached, Lucida thought she'd nip into the office and see what was on offer. She was freelancing for an art-cum-fashion journal that came out of Sydney but had a Perth office. She hated being back in Perth after working in Sydney for two years, and before that, London. She was twenty-six and felt as if opportunities were running away from her. She'd done the hard yards, and here she was messing with old addictions, spending a night here and there with old lovers, and still getting about in her tatty jeans and cheap shoes. Not that she was interested in designer stuff and labels, not that she cared about her grooming or looks – who she was defined itself against these irrelevancies – but she was getting tired and jaded and wanted fame as much as at any other time in her life.

It was a walk from her flat in East Perth to the office opposite the Entertainment Centre, but not a long one. She could have caught the train but it was hardly worth it. She needed to think, she needed to plan. Walking past Queen's Gardens she saw a rat poke its head out of the greenery pressed against the external fence, a day rat, and she smiled at it. Weird. And zig-zagging further on, passing Wellington Square, she saw the latest intake of the Central Drug Unit doing their shamble across the grass to the delicatessen where they would buy their smokes and lollies and chips. An outing. She'd been there, done that. She didn't recognise any of them. In the far corner of the park near Silver City, a Noongar family were arguing with what she knew were Australia First racists. It was an ongoing battle. She felt angry and thought about going over

and having a go at the white nationalists, but then she shrugged
her shoulders and felt good that she was over her period. Periods
annoyed her but were thankfully short. Despite her *curves*, as her
many male bosses and a few female bosses had called them, she
felt more boy than girl and her body annoyed her. She generally
tried not to think about it.

Fame. What is the nature of fame? In London, she'd hung out
with band after band. She'd hung out with writers and painters.
She'd hung out. Interviewing. Writing for fanzines. And then her
youth working visa ran out. Home. Then Sydney and hanging
out and doing the same thing and still no fame. Default setting
Perth. She didn't want to think of family, her *family*. She'd long
abandoned them. She liked to assure herself that they'd abandoned
her. Who were they? People. People who told her to get down
from the tree in her dress as it wasn't seemly *at her age*. People who
made her climb out of her bedroom window at night to meet with
friends. Who fed her 'good food,' who wouldn't let her smoke or
drink at home. Who were always protesting against this or that.

She walked on past Royal Perth hospital which always gave her
the creeps like something out of Mussolini's Rome, and then past
the Red Cross and the Army Surplus Store where she'd bought
her first pair of Doc Martens back when she cared about labels.
And she who wrote, sometimes, occasionally, for a fashion magazine, couldn't give a damn about one label or the next. And yet,
even if she didn't utter their names, she knew them all and how
their designers and makers and marketeers had got them where
they were now. But this was in the silent part of her brain and no
one was going to get access unless it became essential and useful.
And she wasn't going to promote any other label other than her
own, which one day she'd have, a label for everything. It would
be a 'this-that' label and would be numerically mass-produced as
totality. 'This-that' and 'en-bloc.' They would be the subsets of
LUCIDA INTERVALLA. They would disintegrate and be remade
year after year. She would be in a constant cycle of renewal.

And on past the railway station where street kids were fight-
ing each other and spitting at cops and on to the lights at the
Horse Shoe Bridge and its sarcastic swans and her crossing over,

jaywalking, a bus honking its horn at her and getting back a Fuck YOU! Near the office. A spring in her step. The door's electric eye signals her approach and the glass slides open and Alice behind the receptionist's desk says, as she always does, I am just filling in today . . . Ms Ellison is in her office. And through to Ms Ellison who is Zampatti all over and covered in sores where she has worried skin blemishes into volcanoes and bolgias of Inferno. She has a copy of *Cosmo* in front of her which she flicks and hits and speaks to. Without looking up, she says, Lucida, I have a job for you, a special . . . She always called something out of the ordinary 'special' . . . I mean, really special. We're flying you to Centralia where you'll hire a vee-hickle (she was – long, long ago – from Ohio), and go out to The Lake and find Duke in his shack and interview him. He has refused all interviews for years and on the two or three occasions pretty young women have gone out to entice him they have failed. One never came back. Lost out there somewhere, I guess. Anyway, it struck me that you might be a different proposition altogether. A little more savvy. Less preoccupied with yourself. Not so very pretty. So go, and get us the interview that will give this mag the boost it needs. Fucking *Cosmo*, I hate it, she said, pushing it off the desk and into a rubbish bin positioned just for that action.

Lucida stood and stared out the window behind Ms Ellison. My reality is for-itself, she said, watching the bubble burst over the concrete wall opposite. The buildings were close or adjoined and the light was brutal. She saw a seagull fly through the narrow space. She smiled to herself, a deadly smile, and she felt Ms Ellison look up, picking her face, and Lucida, for once, felt shame. Shame of herself and in herself. Before Ms Ellison said a word Lucida was out of there, speaking to Alice about finances and tickets. Alice was in the know, she was always ad-hoc in the know. Alice was excited. This is your big break, Lucida. And she said this without resentment. Lucida stroked Alice's shoulder like a pussy cat, and wondered why she'd felt that little twinge, that small shame. She had everything to be confident about. She swore she'd never acknowledge shame again. She was going to end her ennui, her ongoing 'state of disturbance.'

Let's Start at the Beginning

THIS IS THE beginning. Duke is pulling on his boots, about to step out into the muddy interior. It's not usually muddy, but dusty, this interior, this vast bed of an inland sea. But there had been torrential rain in the north and the sea was refilled, though now it is in full retreat and is muddy. The vast flotillas of waterbirds are a distant cry now, though the odd black-winged stilt pokes around here and there, and the parrots that managed to cope, to persist, in the seemingly eternal – is nothing eternal? – dry have resumed their pokings about, looking for the seed that's sprouted and been drowned with no returns. This isn't what it's about, he thought, sticking his fingers up into a hole and moving a piece of plastic he has slotted in there. The mud'll ooze in but it has been doing so for a while. He doesn't really care. What's he running away from? you ask. Nothing, nothing at all.

He is an artist and he should be in his prime. This once-every-decade event should have been what he was waiting for, but his brushes dried with the wet and he's not even done a sketch. It's gone, whatever he had and whatever he'd hoped for. In the open, he is confined. In the open, and the blue sky, he is isolated. The birds are thoughts flitting by, or pecking at their stems. The heat haze shimmering within a few metres is the mirage he'll never reach, never have. He dehydrates himself as a confrontation with mortality – though a tankerload of fresh water reaches him every few months and, spending his money on little else other than water, food and art supplies, he can afford to bring it in by the tankerload. But the flooding shifted the confinement, and indoors became larger than outside. The deadly hot (and cold at night) corrugated iron, lined with stray sheets of plasterboard and double-layered stretches of hessian, became his event horizon. In there he remembers long left or lost relationships. How many of them have failed due to his poor sense of irony – his inability to recognise what sounds ironic coming from him, and to identify what irony actually is coming from someone else. He wonders about the nuances between sincerity and irony and sarcasm. Does one have to be inside the system to ironise it? Do semantics rule our relationships? Does one person's 'sure' as affirmation come across to another as 'so what'? Isn't it a case of tone? Aren't words vehicles . . . vectors for music? A loud, shrill fast . . . noise . . . isn't the same as a tempered even-paced scale from C . . . surely, sure . . . sure.

He felt in his shed that he'd lost his bearings. Were they dingoes howling? He'd never noticed them before. Wild dogs . . . dingo crosses? He only felt vaguely threatened, and looked up into the moon and then onto the sheen of salt crystals=- where the inland sea had been. There were no people now, no outsiders. And yet he had been reminded that he didn't belong. But surely . . . by his breathing and forgetting and dying here, they wouldn't be able to erase his presence. For then and always.

The woman came to interview him – arrived in her four-wheel-drive with enough water to refill the lake, with a satellite phone, with his mail collected from the last town before the trek out *here*. He ignored her and flicked through letter after letter – advantages of no email. Print. Script. And packages of paint supplies and books. A box of dried flowers to remind him of more temperate zones in the south, but the driedness seemed a vision of the future. He might as well burn here first. Soon, no floods would come, or they'd come once more and take him away, and he'd die there, but his body would rest far away. Then he asked her, straight-faced (as straight as his parched and damaged face could make itself), with all the sincerity he could muster, Are you sure you want to be here? Sorry? Wait a minute, I think I left the stereo running in the vehicle . . . I can hear Sonic Youth's *Dirty* playing. Excuse me for a sec . . . can't afford to get a flat battery out here! And she was out the shack door . . . he listened hard and couldn't hear a thing . . . her shoes were silent across the ground and not even a bird called out. Nothing, nothing at all. And what was dirty?

Lucida

HER NAME WAS Lucida. Is that for real? he asked, pouring her a cup of tea. Black tea. Yes, she said. It was Genevieve but I changed it to Lucida because adults named me. He stared into his enamel mug and wondered why he'd given her his only china cup and saucer.

When I was in Mauritius, she started to say, and he looked past her permed hair into the light, the openness, and wondered why people had to always be somewhere else. Where they had been, where they were going. He guessed he smelt and was filthy and that she'd rather be somewhere close to the sea, or dunking in and out of waves – not too rough, just gentle consistent lapping waves.

Was she looking under the table at his feet – to see if his boots were really boots? Or maybe at the bathroom scales he'd pushed under there when she arrived. The relic of an old relationship when he'd had to watch his weight . . . where he'd *had* to watch his weight. Do they work? she asks. What? Your scales? What an odd thing to have all the way out here, where there's no television and no computer and no telephone. He wondered what the correlation between these objects and his scales might be. Yes, they work. Can I use them? she asked. I'm a sucker for a set of scales.

FALLOUT

It spread like a teardrop northwest across country. Duke told her he couldn't help but be conscious of this. But that wouldn't have affected *here*, she said. All of us have been affected. Whole peoples were driven out and the cleanup is only about return in a surface-way. Of course, in a surface-sense, they were always there, even at Ground Zero. Emu Plains. But seriously, she added, that's a different zone, a different region so far from here. All of us have a glimmer of plutonium embedded in who we are. Fuel cell to the soul? she joked. Ah, he said aloud, the tyranny of irony. How far is this going to go? I don't want to be seduced. Visibly pulling back and clutching her recording device to her chest, she said, Gee, mate, you've got tabs on yourself . . . I was told you weren't like that. A eunuch, almost. Almost, he replied sadly or glibly.

She slept cramped and cooped up in the back of her four-wheel-drive. In the morning, Duke broke free of the shack, and walked away from it and her car into the lake bed – still tacky, though not really muddy. Dust prevalent. A slight *crunch crunch* as he broke through here and there. From deeper inland he saw a flight of confused and come-from-nowhere pelicans heading adjacent to the sun, south. Small patches of crisped wildflowers around his shack, those sent in a box, the draining of a large part of Australia, explorers imagining boats left stranded where they lost their support . . . he remembered the thousands of ibises. Their curved beaks, the rush of paintings that suddenly repelled him. Across the floodplain. Dingoes, yes, curling away into hollows that had filled and were now dry. Pups. Post- the time of plenty . . . stray cows with calves, nibbling at the thin sheen of dead grass soon to be skin and bones, the birds of prey . . . the legacy lingers like fallout.

Lucida found Duke sitting in the crystals and dirt. She sat down beside him, turned on her recording device, and asked, Is this how you get your inspiration? A hissing silence filled the recording and she reassured herself she had plenty of charged batteries and the hiss could be edited out of the silence. Textually, she could write 'SILENCIO' or 'nothingness' or 'blank' in the transcript. Then, finally, he said, See the hawk in the distance, just hanging there. Early morning thermals. Oh, she said. Do you know, I haven't had *real* sex since Ben dumped me outside the Adelaide Festival Centre? I think we were going to see something by Beckett. He used my ticket for someone else – I handed it over without too much of a fuss. Some things just run their course. Did she expect Duke – the artiste – to turn to her and say, Lucida, you are a remarkable woman? To ask her what constituted *real* sex? Precedent – from her life's journeying – might suggest so, but then again, the rules of social interaction were probably skewed out there for people of all backgrounds. *Silencio.* I like my space in the mornings, Lucida . . . let me have that and we might find room for talk. There's not a lot of space free for idle chatter out here.

Conception Art

I WOULD LIKE to conceive at sunset, anyway, said Lucida. A
sunset baby. And so, he painted her at sunset, over the six days
of creation. On the seventh they shared their water as if on the
desert planet of Dune. I think that's his best film . . . even better
than *Blue Velvet*, she said. Especially the scene where Kyle rides
the worm and his gang of stillsuiters join in. You've got to love
the thumpers. Just roos and rabbits and dingoes and camels
mammal-wise here, he said, struggling to maintain momentum,
never mind climb the hill of denial. Out here, she said, you've
always got the feeling someone is watching . . . I mean the walls
of this stinking shack are thin. And it's so fucking hot in the day,
even at this supposedly milder time of the year, and the nights
are like a freezer. I don't know how you manage with two army
blankets . . . what will you do without me to snuggle up to you,
bunny-like?

'Seven-Tongued Orator'

READERS OF PROSE (fiction) feel cheated by strings of short lines, she said. Picking at the hessian, examining it closer than her eyesight allowed, she added, It's been seven years since your last exhibition . . . do you think the Conception series might be the core of your next, that it might be sooner than later?

She was almost growing used to his long, sweaty silences. I could be useful to you if you took a new and fresh exhibition o/s, she said. I speak Japanese, Indonesian, Malay, French, Italian and Spanish. I could be most . . . useful.

Do you like soul singing? she asked. The shack stank of white spirits. He was cleaning brushes. She wanted to say, Can't you do that outside, but wasn't confident she was quite there yet . . . What on earth was she thinking? She wasn't laying claim and no one was claiming her. But nonetheless, she did want to know . . . Do you like soul . . . and, Gee that stinks, in a kind of throwaway laughing voice that couldn't be misconstrued as an attempt to control her own environment, for since she had moved in out of her car it was as much her environment as his. Don't mind it, he said, and kept at his brushes. Then he said, and you could have knocked her over with a feather – Not that I believe in souls, not really. She felt this statement was a violent act and resolved to leave as soon as possible, to alter the conditions of their unspoken contract. But now rather than later . . . when it was *too late*. Don't judge me too harshly, she told her conscience, you and I have no idea what he is capable of. Only a misogynist would live out here alone in this way. Then she wondered if she had enough material for her interview, and resolved to hang around for a few days more. He was so funny about water – a person had to bathe!

CLOUDS

HE DIDN'T PROTEST her leaving but he truly missed her. It wasn't like him to make things up, say things he didn't believe, but he heard himself whispering over and over in the star-wrecked darkness, the window open to emptiness, that he believed in souls, loved souls, lived for souls. And then unseasonal . . . unheard of CLOUDS swept in and wrapped him up in stories he'd never been told but suddenly knew intimately and sincerely. He grew impatient when a textual-artist-scientist fella turned up and basically invited himself, bunking down on the spare cot. Duke listened to this pedantic bastard snoring and to his bullshit about how connected he felt to the land while taking data and how he was due for promotion and that he'd read that interview in the glossy pages of the Oz's liftout . . . about his relationship . . . *your* relationship with space and silence and absence and presence and all of that. Would you have any objections to my doing a bit of photographing in and around the shack, I've some *really good* stuff generating inside . . . ? I too have creative bones in my body. And so on and on and on and on.

Oh, Rodger Dodger (it had snuck out, and devastated her!), I would simply and absolutely and wonderfully and deliciously be fucking excited and welcome it with open and generous arms! He called on Lucida's absent alter ego for a dose of irony, for support.

Duke took hold of his canvases and holding them in an ungainly and fateful way, stomped out towards the eye of water hundreds of ks away now. The scientist with artistic pretensions pursued him.

You going walkabout? Rodger Dodger (there was no keeping him in place, he was out of the locker) yelled behind him. Was this irony? Was Rodger entirely stone? His name was really Benji, Duke knew. He was a famous academic, a university citizen who produced vast amounts of research kudos for his institution. He had betrayed his friend Ben, though Ben had only been mentioned in a whisper. Or had he said over a joint that his best friend had been called Benji and that he'd stolen all his best ideas from him? Duke was getting paranoid, walking and stumbling and dropping canvases like confetti, remembering snippets of overlong and strained conversations with Lucida. He felt guilty – once he had started talking he couldn't stop. Or stop enough. And she could talk the proverbial hind leg off . . . and she went on and on about her 'history.' He remembered some of it. What was that dickhead (was that really what he thought of him), yelling about the *Never Never* and those fucking insulting, stupid and insulting Gormley installations. What was it? Where was Lucida these days . . . enjoying the fruits of her damage?

My Oath

Observing the poverty of wit, he deployed the road signs as his makers instructed. Employment is a privilege, they had drilled into him and his brethren, each and every one of them full of the zest of imitation.

Such was the mode of utterance that she accepted his tragedy and moved on. Birds of the agon bristled with rage and hunger and yet ignored the feast spread out below them, choosing instead the thinnest lands.

And taking the plot as a stimulus to action, they took strides across the dry places pissing down a plethora of ambiguities. Stylish and perfect even their enemies claimed in write-ups birthed of good faith.

This epic story nudges towards tragedy, DADA magic exclusive love word beautiful as deprivation art requiring an action to shouting nostalgia and neurotic impositions to mean the nothing of all-ness. But Lucida was part of his

art of absence now. She had, by default, become the artist herself. She met with friends at a well-known Adelaide coffee house to let them know she was moving into the next phase of her life. There would be no room for trivialities, no room

for friends. She needed space, wide spaces in which to work. I am going to work out near Maralinga, she told them, and when the dropped jaws exclaimed, 'What about the radiation!' she merely said, I have applied through the right channels and

have permission. I have the authority. I have my mother tongue and I am taking it into the zone of other languages, which I will attempt to learn over time. I will paint these words. She sipped her mochaccino and stared at the table with

gravitas, thinking through the stunned silence (an otherwise empty shop), that she had indeed surmounted yet another peak in her quest. She, too, was a Christian. She half-wondered if her cluster of friends would ritualistically . . .

lament her passing into another state of being. She took out her iPad and brought up Jowett's translation of Plato's *The Republic* and went to Book V and highlighted a dialogue and passed the tablet to her left where it was dutifully examined

and then passed left again until it had come full circle. It goes:

> Well, I replied, I suppose that I must retrace my steps and say what I perhaps ought to have said before in the proper place. The part of the men has been played out, and now

> properly enough comes the turn of the women. Of them I will proceed to speak, and the more readily since I am invited by you. For men born and educated like our citizens, the only way, in my opinion, of arriving at a right conclusion about

> the possession and use of women and children is to follow the path on which we originally started, when we said that the men were to be the guardians and watchdogs of the herd. True. Let us further suppose the birth and education of

our women to be subject to similar or nearly similar regu-
lations; then we shall see whether the result accords with
our design. What do you mean? What I mean may be
put into the form of a question, I said: Are dogs divided

into *hes* and *shes*, or do they both share equally in hunting
and in keeping watch and in the other duties of dogs? Or
do we entrust to the males the entire and exclusive care
of the flocks, while we leave the females at home, under
the idea

that the bearing and suckling their puppies is labour
enough for them? No, he said, they share alike; the only
difference between them is that the males are stronger and
the females weaker. But can you use different animals for
the same

purpose, unless they are bred and fed in the same way?
You cannot.
Then, if women are to have the same duties as men, they
must have the same nurture and education? Yes. The education which was assigned to the men was

music and gymnastics. Yes. Then women must be taught
music and gymnastic and also the art of war, which they
must practise like the men? That is the inference, I suppose. I should rather expect, I said, that several of our

proposals, if they are carried out, being unusual, may
appear ridiculous. No doubt of it. Yes, and the most ridiculous thing of all will be the sight of women naked in the
palaestra, exercising with the men, especially when they
are no

longer young; they certainly will not be a vision of beauty,
any more than the enthusiastic old men who in spite of
wrinkles and ugliness continue to frequent the gymnasia.

Yes, indeed, he said: according to present notions the proposal

would be thought ridiculous. But then, I said, as we have determined to speak our minds, we must not fear the jests of the wits which will be directed against this sort of innovation; how they will talk of women's attainments both in music

and gymnastic, and above all about their wearing armour and riding upon horseback!

And with that, Lucida noisily pushed her chair back, said, Later, girls . . . and departed the scene.

A Seducer's Notebook

30 AND LOT WENT up out of Zoar, and dwelt in the mountain, and his two daughters with him; for he feared to dwell in Zoar: and he dwelt in a cave, he and his two daughters.

31 And the firstborn said unto the younger, Our father is old, and there is not a man in the earth to come in unto us after the manner of all the earth:

32 Come, let us make our father drink wine, and we will lie with him, that we may preserve seed of our father.

33 And they made their father drink wine that night: and the first-born went in, and lay with her father; and he perceived not when she lay down, nor when she arose.

34 And it came to pass on the morrow, that the firstborn said unto the younger, Behold, I lay yesternight with my father: let us make him drink wine this night also; and go thou in, and lie with him, that we may preserve seed of our father.

35 And they made their father drink wine that night also: and the younger arose, and lay with him; and he perceived not when she lay down, nor when she arose.

36 Thus were both the daughters of Lot with child by their father.

37 And the first born bare a son, and called his name Moab: the same is the father of the Moabites unto this day.

38 And the younger, she also bare a son, and called his name Benammi: the same is the father of the children of Ammon unto this day.

But Lucida knew that she had no child in her belly. But she knew a homunculus had been implanted and would grow there never to be birthed. It would reach into her circulatory system and into her nervous system, and lay claim. But Lucida was stronger than it and would fight for control and make it do her bidding. She was prepared. She had been waiting for this since the first adults 'helped' her before she had words and who had offered her words that would help *them* control *her.* She knew the tricks and the ruses, she knew Duke and his DNA hijinks. She would not let him be taken into the future without her having the final say, the final disruption and if necessary erasure of code.

Lucida Desires Danish Citizenship

DESPITE BECOMING A full bottle on Tal R's *kolbojnik*, they turned her down. She regretted not expounding on Hammershøi as it was the act of turning the outdoors indoors that was becoming her signature. A tin shack with a simple wooden cross above a single iron bed and the ghost of the Duke hovering upright or prostrate in the room above the bed, outside the window. Was it a supernatural motif, or something else. She called it a form of domestic realism, an examination of role play. In these works I protest my innocence, she said to the young man who came to interview her, staying only a few hours before doing the long drive back to Port Augusta where he overnighted, then on to Adelaide to file his story which was something of a scoop. Lucida was considered 'shy' and 'eccentric' in Australia, though she had a massive following in Scandinavia.

But when Lucida read the article, she said to herself and the two women elders who were staying in the shack for a couple of nights with her while their men were further south, That young fella – that journo or scientist or artist or whatever he was – misrepresented me. That's not *me* in that article. And they said, We know. They were Christians as well, but didn't say anything about divine Governance. She wanted to paint them under the cross, sitting looking out the side of their eyes to the vast, full emptiness. It's good that you've got tanks of water out here, one of the women said to her. Yes, I spend the money I earn on water. Soon, I am going to paint water. Just arid zones and water and radiation. Yes, the women said together, generations suffer. Yes, said Lucida, when I went back out to Centralia to visit Duke, to interview him a second time, to see how he'd progressed in my absence, I told him that he needed more water tanks. He *never* bathed you know, other than on those rare occasions the lake flooded or a sea swept him away.

The Ghost of Duke Hovers over the Old Iron Bed

IT WAS A shack (the uprights were cut from the last remaining tree of the before-desert – the only tree that didn't burn down to the roots: the 'anomalous tree' it was called – it had blown down during a storm and was divided up into many parts adding up to more than the sum of its original self), made in the image of himself. The distance between Duke and Lucida was immense, but they shared much, especially after a separation and reconnecting. Especially because she'd come to him of her own volition, and without a magazine paying her expenses. Duke felt it was the magnetic qualities of his bedstead that drew her to him, the shack, Centralia.

Can you dream when you're dead, when you're a phantom? Duke was dreaming of that post-porn queen of pleasure, Annie Sprinkle. Now she was an eco-post-porn queen. He wanted to cuddle her. He'd become cuddly in the afterlife. He hadn't the slightest interest in cuddling Lucida who had quickly become as cold as the desert night in the outrageous sun of noontime. How in such heat could a person be so buttoned up? He floated there, above the bed, a good model, keeping the same pose as she painted. Actually, even if he wanted to flex a muscle, show her his chunky biceps, nothing would happen. There was a disconnection. Sex, for him, had never been about connecting. What was it for Lucida? She seemed so clinically indifferent, so bored with it all. And was there a child? Did she miscarry?

He should know these things being now so very dead and having access to all the hiding places of the world. He was slightly amused, reading over the shoulder of an old academic somewhere (where was he, really, at any given time? – posing for Lucida, filling in the spaces between worshippers on their mats, in their pews, walking through temples, lighting incense, having shouts at demonstrations amplify through his ectoplasm?) that interaction in the time of social media was 'ambient intimacy,' that all were ghosts without borders, eavesdropping with permission on someone's ablutions . . . paradox had ceased to exist. Duke felt alive in the afterlife of all existence. The living were already dead and the explosion of technology was a manifestation of pure grit Thanatos. Duke was suddenly flatulent, and Lucida in her coldness still registered a slight relief that a cool breeze lifted her wispy hair. A cold blowing from nowhere, she thought. We are never alone. But she didn't care why Duke was hovering there or where the wind came from, just that it was there. Later, a young woman who has shed her piercings and had the butterfly on her *mons veneris* removed by a deftly wielded laser, will call this the Fresh Teleology, the 'new' having well and truly been ditched in that phase of non-corporeality.

Duke waits for rains that will never come. Why is it she's painting me naked? he wondered. Am I not clothed in the very clothes I passed away in? He tries to examine himself but comes to no firm conclusion. Shit, am I dressed or am I undressed? For a nanosecond he darts behind Lucida and notices she is adding grey hairs to his scrotum. He feels embarrassed. There he is, all floppy and shrunken and . . . passive. Was this how she sees him – had seen him – during their brief time together? He flashes back into position and stares into the nothingness that is his essence.

Fuck! shrieked (yelled?) Lucida, who then stabbed the canvas with the brush repeatedly. Hoy! Duke tried to yell, feeling every blow. What had happened? What had snapped? Now Lucida was kicking the canvas, oils all over her sandshoes. Fuckfuckfuckfuckfuck! And that was it. She gave no further clues. He slid out of her life, once and for all!

The Duke Banishes Himself to Copenhagen

ARRIVING AT VESTERBROGADE 59, 1620 København V, he popped in after hours and slipped into Søren's clothes. After 200 years the jester philosopher had grown weary of them. They were, it might be said, up for grabs as long as nobody noticed.

Continuum

AND THUS IT came to pass and the distance was greater for its narrowing. A conjoining, a breathing in of the atoms of demise, made dead seed take shape, spread its tentacles. If Lucida was indirectly speaking to post-Duke she was also asking simple questions of herself. Could she be ETERNALLY birthing without the satisfaction of nurture? She had no female friends left to speak of, but if she did, surely they'd be asking if she now felt *fulfilled*? Full, yes, dearies, she would say. She was prepared. It is the sensuousness of the fringe, she recited, it is the bliss of ennui, it is the cradle of souls dropped out of the programme. This birth always happening that is no birth, this authorship of annex and verandah I will never sign off on. She laid herself bare, she consumed the desert winds, she laughed in the face of her own dentate. This is my self-marriage and marriage with self. When Dennis Hopper's Frank sends a love letter, we know how it will end. Lucida had watched *Blue Velvet* thirteen times in a row and had written the script – the chatter – out from memory. This care of my soul, my message in a bottle, my saying goodbye to aloneness, no longer blind on the catwalk. This escape from the gravitational poll of evil. From the feminine possessive. So what's missing from my argument, Roger (Cebes?)? I see you are all full of doubt, birds of the desert, birds of the night, parrots of the ground. Is this my misfortune? Should I tell you so? Or an opportunity, birds, or an opportunity?

Lucida Back from Centralia (Again) is a Changed Person

DUKE IS DEAD, she began her intro to The Final Interview. I cannot say how he died, because I do not know, but he vanished into the desert. I know in my bones that he is dead. I have been through police interview after police interview, there has been search after search. Trackers have been deployed. But he is nowhere. I interviewed him. He mentioned how sick of fame he was, and he walked off into the night. I am not under suspicion. Duke's struggle with depression was well known and it was a fact he was off his medication. That he'd some years earlier been living in a community that was shut down through government cutting services, that he'd had some issues with the authorities over his resistance to their intrusions, is also well known. He went off by himself, built a shack from corrugated iron. Sustained an existence in solitude looking for an extinct bird species and painting ephemeral works that left no trace after a few days. More 'permanent' works have been lost. But I was fortunate to see him at work and photograph some of these incredible moments. In a few weeks spread over two visits I got to know him well. He asked *me* to watch over his legacy, he, in a word, anointed me. We bonded. We became more than the sum of our parts. Now, he speaks through me.

*

At first, she had to confront negative even malicious reviews. She

64

was called ignorant, a rip-off, and shallow. It was said she had no
knowledge of art or art history, that she was merely an opportunist. Occasionally, it was hinted that she might be a murderer, but
not often, as Lucida was a fast learner and had engaged the best
QC in the business who leapt on such utterances with glee and
made both Lucida and himself a packet in the process. Lucida
didn't mind the negative publicity, and took on an agent and
publicist to generate activity when blanks and silences appeared
on the event horizon. She was becoming famous. Let them all
accuse her of not understanding fame. She would redefine the
price of fame. She was in herself [itself] a cause she was finding. She had read enough on ontology between gigs to get this.
Where there were gaps in her knowledge she would make a new
lexicon, a new nomenclature. She would define the terms, or
redefine old terms if they already existed which Lucida admitted
was likely. But a new wheel is a new wheel and it rolls on just
fine. She quickly developed a set of stock epithets to see her
through the pressure of this period in her cycle of life dominance.
She said things like, Well, it's all chicken and egg, isn't it. Or,
You've got to start somewhere. Or, I've got the world by the short
and curlies. Or, That's just banana logic. Or, I am reinventing
the stunner as object. Or, A photo tells a thousand truths. Or,
Painting is all in the wrist. Over many long lunches, her *elderly*
lawyer agreed. It's all in the wording, he'd say, rubbing her leg
which she only half liked but tolerated for the time being. I think
I need a workshop, she said. You know, workers. Yes, that can
be set up, he said. It will all be in the paperwork. I only want
young men to work for me, she said, And I don't want any of
them to use their names in my presence. They will simply be The
Boys. Automatons. They will do as I say, fulfil my every wish
and command. They must also be supremely talented and know
everything there is about art and art history. They must know
heaps about chiaroscuro which I have always found difficult but
I feel will be essential to my work. They must bathe regularly.
I am, after all, a wonderful agreement of light and shade. You
are, Lucida, you are, her lawyer fawned. He knew the future
when it was there before his eyes, under his sweaty palm, his

gold-ringed fingers.

*

Ms Ellison never completely understood how she lost control of
the Duke interview material. You gave me a snippet, she opined,
and did a deal with *Cosmo* for the rest. What on earth has *Cosmo*
to do with art? Do you remember Vivienne Westwood? asked
Lucida.

*

Lucida kept one keepsake from her time with Duke that she
never told anyone about. In fact, she buried it in a special place,
though that place would eventually go under the water with the
rising sea. It would remain buried in her head, and there she
occasionally accessed it. It was a 2B pencil with which he did
a small portrait of her before burning the drawing with a Bic
lighter he'd borrowed from her to show her the true value of
art. She wept inside but didn't show him she cared. At the time,
she couldn't reconcile the act with how much the piece would
have been worth, but in retrospect it made good fiscal sense.
Ephemeral art. Duke had dropped the pencil into a tin with
dozens of others but she had watched it fall into place with laser
eyes and retrieved it and stashed it away in the vee-hee-ickle. It
was her talisman. Her first label would be her name with a pencil
in her delicate hand in place of the 'i': LUC✏DA.

*

Lucida visited the Stoned Crow one last time before closing the
door on that part of her life. She carried a small phial of amyl
nitrate and went to hear her favourite local punk band. She
went with her old friend the speed dealer, The Professor. She had
tried to find Ben, but Ben was elsewhere. Maybe trekking in the
Himalayas on a shoestring. The Professor was always wanting
Lucida and had tried to blackmail her into sex with him, but
having failed, just followed her like a puppy dog now. In his
big black trench coat and trying to play teacher to the girls just

out of high school, the first and second year uni girls looking for street cred and bohemian angst to shit their parents off in the polite riverside suburbs. The Professor occasionally supplied these 'nubiles' with bad trips that had them so terrified that he nurtured them into awareness. But such things didn't work on Lucida. She was a veteran.

Lucida said Hi! to the barmaid who was a sort of friend from way back, and asked for two Kirup Syrups. Maybe this would be the last rotgut she ever drank. She could feel wealth approaching. But Kirup was a rite de passage, and she wasn't quite ready to outstrip her subcultural roots. The band, King Pig, were insane on the small stage, and The Professor was in there slamming with the young 'uns. Lucida, in her torn Levis and The Damned t-shirt, sat on a stool and looked for a target to share a blast of amyl with. She eyed off a young woman who looked like she was in the wrong scene, with a pencil skirt and boots and a denim jacket and one side of her hair cut short the other hanging over her eye. Lucida, with what she called her 'pastoral care stare' drew the woman to her side. Producing the phial, she yell-whispered over the thrashing guitar and hammering drums, Want a sniff? What is it? came the yell back. Amyl, darl.

*

Music. What of it? The music of the spheres is what she heard playing in the yellow sand down behind the shed when she was five. She is digging holes and filling them with water from her seaside bucket. It is a long long walk, a walk of forever, back to the tap to fill the bucket. She should save the water, use little portions for her experiments, but she can't help herself and pours it all into the crumbling yellow holes to watch them dissolve and collapse and the water vanish. Her bucket is red with white plastic flowers adorning it, and the flowers are crumbling because the bucket has spent too much time in the sun and it's that kind of plastic. She rubs the crumbling dusty plastic and it coats her hand which she must taste. Yellow and plastic dust. She will get the collywobbles. Someone is calling her to come in and wash up for lunch. She has a white hat on and her head is hot. She is burning and the water has gone.

*

There is an aviary full of parrots and quail on the ground and mouse holes because the mice come for the birdseed and water. Her fingers through the wire, someone says, Watch out or those noisy parrots will snip your fingers off, Lucida. Parrots have never snipped my fingers before, says Lucida. They say, Giggle giggle whenever they open their beaks. They do poops on the quail that run around down below on the ground. Don't speak like that, Lucida, it's dirty talk! I'll wash your mouth out with soap if you speak like that again. Speak like that. Again. *Giggle giggle* go the parrots who will snip your fingers tips off, snip snip snip, and poop on the quail while doing it.

Lucida Protests Her Innocence

WHY ALL THESE years later she was still suspected of foul play in the passing of the artist known as Duke was a mystery. There was no cold case evidence, just innuendo in the press, likely emanating (like putrid malformed ripples) from that filthy narcissistic young male arts journalist who'd tried to score a second interview with her and take a sidetour of her vagina but had been sent away with a flea in his ear. The seeding article was entitled, *Voss?* She laughed to herself and thought it a joke, but at the same time, she was pretty sure she was being watched. She could never pin things down – rather, it was a feeling. Someone over her shoulder, even, like morgellons, outside pathology but in there, under the skin. Offered a massive commission to paint Lucas Heights, she embraced the reactor and spent months behind the security fences [naively] painting ghostly figures going about their business. She was fascinated by medical isotopes and felt they were somehow tied to her fate. Maybe this wasn't so unusual. She regretted attacking that ghost portrait of Duke, but given it was the hundredth she'd done, she'd just flipped out. A bad trip. And that's what the little bastard, that metrosexual journo, homed in on. Why so many portraits of a dead man? Why was she reproducing his modus operandi. Fool, she wasn't. She called out to Duke inside the control room of the reactor, but he was nowhere. Nowhere near. What would Duke have said about her present commission? She had no idea in a personal sense but in researching him for her original article – the progenitor of it all – she had come across photographs of him shaking his fist during anti-nuclear warship marches in Fremantle. There he was, all dressed in jute and withy bare feet, the strains of Kathmandu and the Pudding Shop in his dreadlocks . . . She was pretty sure, he'd be turning in his grave if he had any interest in her at all. Maybe that's why she was doing it – to rouse him out of his sleep, to bring back the vengeful God looking to punish and haunt her. Lucida let loose! Lucida, the brightest girl in her year at school, committing magic realist suicide. She looked around – the technicians were at their panels and computers and the reactor was humming along sweetly.

Lucida's Once-Best Friend Raises a Child Possibly Not Her Own

HILDA RAISED THE boy Marcel as her own. A robust baby, he grew into a rambunctious toddler, an inquisitive preschooler, a bemused primary-schooler, a bullied lower-high-schooler and a truant upper-high-schooler. But maybe we're getting ahead of ourselves, because he's no more than eight years of age now and wondering why Hilda flinches every time he says, Mummy. He loves Hilda; he aches with love for Hilda. He would spend all his time with her if he could. And she clearly loves him, wrapping him up in cotton wool, encouraging his softer side. He likes drawing with pastels but nothing else. Just pastels. Coloured pencils still make him cry. One day Mummy's friend Lucida visited from 'the country' and gave him a box of watercolour paints. He tried to smile at her and couldn't. Lucida shrugged her shoulders and said, Just like his father, which Marcel didn't understand because he hadn't been aware that he'd ever had a father and didn't especially want one. This 'lack' will cause him little stress in his adult life when he will hold down a ten-to-four government job, raise three children of his own and vote middle-ground Green. As a father himself, he will love Hilda as much as he did as a child, and still wonder why she grimaced when he said, Mummy, which he will still do constantly. After years of talking it over with his wife, a psychologist, they will decide Hilda has a nervous tic and no doubt the frequency of his 'Mummy' set her off. He will change his mannerism to a low guttural *M-o-t-h-e-r*, and the tic, sure enough and Bob's your uncle, stopped. Lovely to see you, Mother . . . Sometimes things take an awful long time to sink in, he joked to his wife after sex one night, sniggering at his own irony, quite overwhelmingly impressed with himself. It should be said that his wife laughed too. Theirs was a beautiful marriage or maybe mirage until the children were grown and at university, when they started hating each other with such a vengeance that they concluded they'd not shared a single good moment together and that it had been complete exploitation (each exploiting the other, depending on point of view), and that something had clearly gone subliminally wrong in his – according to her – and her – according to him – childhood. But they will stick together in their bitterness and die within a few weeks of each other. Their ghosts will rest quite peaceably, actually.

Swapping Stories

I SAID TO Lucida, Let's swap stories from our childhood. She agreed and said, You go first. So I did, honestly so. She'd see right through me if I made it up. I don't mind giving a bit of who I am to – help. Help open her up. She's such a closed book. So I told her about putting my mouth around a drainpipe and getting worms. My mother had always told me to stay away from the drainpipe that came out of the back of the house from the laundry. It had one of those metal flaps on it – I was fascinated by the way it always had hair and bits of mop hanging from the pipe, under the flap. I would lift the flap and look into its darkness, hoping something would come out. It was actually too big to get my mouth around, and with the flap in the way, beyond the realm of possibility. But I tried – to catch what it had to offer, but also to speak into it, to use it to breathe in all the strange things of the world. And being an honest boy, I told my mum straight away. Or maybe I told her because I knew I might get sick and telling her would ward off the evil. An Anglican confessional – mother in the laundry in the 1960s. And sure enough, I found the wrigglers on the toilet paper and looked into the bowl and saw them white and weaving around the dark poo – water worms. Mum dosed me, and I never did it again. A cautionary tale. I suppose the fact that I 'learnt' from it showed me as 'limited' to Lucida, but she did, nonetheless, tell me a tale of her own, and I believed its provenance and veracity. Maybe you had to be there.

Lucida said: I made an insect collection. You know, I caught and killed insects, stuck them on a polystyrene sheet, and put labels under them. I used pins for the insects and the labels because stickytape wouldn't hold the labels onto the polystyrene. I remember the names more than I do the insects, though maybe I remember the insects' colours most of all. And their shapes. But I have trouble matching the names to the colours and shapes, that's what I am saying. To me it was all about the display, but the fun part was the killing jar. Anyway, I'll get to that in a jiff. The names of insects from the ballast brick and exotic gardens in the well-off suburbs of the wide Adelaide streets and then the Perth south of the river suburbs before all the bush was cleared. Green lacewings, Granny Moth Caterpillar, Mole Cricket, Praying Mantids, Blue Ants and Bristle Flies, Gumleaf Skeletoniser – a favourite – and red-eyed cicadas. But the killing jar. My father made it for me. I didn't hate my father, but I didn't love him either. He was just there sometimes, and told me off, and didn't say much that was positive. But he did approve of my insect board, and the time we spent together was over the killing jar, which he made for me, and let me . . . pilot, as he said. My father was a chemist and had access to potassium cyanide, the fastest killing agent. You might be thinking that I enjoyed watching the insects die? I didn't, though I can't speak for my dad. But I was fascinated by the rapidity of the toxin, and the danger of handling it. I enjoyed manipulating the captured insect – usually beetles and other 'tougher' insects – into the jar, holding my breath, twisting the top on the jar just tight enough. Motor skills, my father called them, standing close behind me, almost inhaling the vapours. It was about the chemistry of death rather than death itself. And you know, I've always thought of art in those terms – as acts of chemistry and physics. But that's just the background to my story. On one occasion I caught a beautiful jewelled beetle and wanted to give it pride of place in my collection. I went to kill it and discovered that the drop of cyanide had lost its oomph – no doubt still deadly, but that beetle crawled around in there as if it was discovering the limits of the world. My dad isn't around and I can't get into his home laboratory, which is locked with double-locks and a deadlock, and the window has a grille across it. So I think to myself, what's as deadly as cyanide? – and my ten-year-old brain decides it's the rank-smelling perfume my mother douses herself with *every time* they go out. I am always getting into trouble for gagging and rolling about when she's got it on, and she says, You'd think it was poison, Lucida, the way you carry on. It *is*, Mum, it is! So I march straight into the house, go to Mum's dresser drawer, find the offending perfume and take it down to the shed and the killing jar. I soak the gauze at the bottom of the jar not with a drop but half the bottle, so it's flooded, then pour the whole mess out into a hole I dig in the sand behind the shed. I find a bit of rag and drop that in the bottom, probably spreading cyanide all over, and then the rest of the bottle of perfume goes in. Another mess. I give in, find another jar and stick the beetle in there and leave it with the lid closed to starve or suffocate or whatever over the next week. The stench is so extreme I vomit. I stink of the stuff. I try to wash the smell away with the garden hose. It won't go. I'm a kid who can handle cyanide but I can't handle my mother's perfume. I am called for dinner and won't go in. I'm busy! I don't care, Missy – I hated how she'd call me Missy – come in and wash up for dinner. Eventually I slink in and all hell lets loose, and that's the end of my insect collecting. I won't bore you with the details, other than to say my father got off scot-free for giving me cyanide to play with, and I told my mum about it and it was like water off a duck's back, just glazed over as if she didn't comprehend a word and maybe she didn't! That perfume costs two hundred dollars an ounce, she *screamed* – it was a gift from your father on our tenth wedding anniversary. You have so disappointed me, young lady, so disappointed me.

Conversion

THE CHURCH ALMOST got hold of her but lost out in the end. A visitor to her own – FINALFINAL – exhibition, she decided to look elsewhere for spiritual solace and certainty. It was simply called *The Duke Show* and was launched with a public séance. She called up the spirit of Duke to prove it existed. He turned up, of course, just a little put out but typically lacklustre. It barely got a mention in the papers as an event which was surprising given that by this stage Lucida controlled much of the conventional media and strongly influenced patterns of social media, though the paintings themselves had the critics drooling. Her conversion was sincere and absolute. She continued her visits to church and to wander its environs. She encountered him and claiming she believed actually believed something else. The pain he was administering was no pain at all. She believed elsewhere. She told her inquisitors that she was born in Copenhagen on the twenty-third of January, 1822, and that she received the letters from her Saviour each Wednesday at roughly the same time of day. Already her self-esteem was being damaged by accusations of predatory amorousness. Seeking happiness, she'd found the monster of communication indirect. *Either/Or. Repetition.* I am a betraying beast, I am the deceiver, I am dropping you, my betrothed. How would you feel? The sanctimonious? The intermediary between Jesus and Kierkegaard himself. God. The town bristled with his cruelty. Celibate faith. Villain. Penitent. Virtue. Solicitude. Black-hearted. She did say: What about *my* predicament? but journalists missed that. But they did quote her as saying, I couldn't give a damn about your systems, I am one with the line . . . I am at one with the blue and the ochre and am full of your God of radiation. I am in the third phase of my life – I embrace my menopause. This statement shocked the boy journalists who spent many words describing Lucida Bright's long and dowdy skirt without out-and-out condemnation. A matter of taste. Of employment. The compromises we make!

Ben and the 'Great Earthquake'

IF BEN WAS an early love of Lucida's, it was Ben's love for Lucida
and its failure that set him free. She had long forgotten him,
enthralled with the ghost of Duke, but he had not forgotten her
and from his hermit's cell watched her every move in and out
of the public eye on his computer screen. But she had been the
cross on his great expectations, she had been his curse. More than
once he'd deleted his hard drive of all pertaining to her, only to
trawl the net and rebuild her profile, to scan old photographs
in, even newsclippings that had not found their way into cyber-
space. When the earthquake hit, it was the loss of power, his
being disconnected from the grid – in fact, the collapse of the
grid – that snapped him. That he ran riot for days, that many
unsolved crimes might be attributed to him, that he looted and
pillaged, seemed entirely logical. Lucida was being held in cus-
tody pending a bail application. She was being charged with
murder. He wouldn't accept it. The fact she'd used and sold LSD
in her 'university years' wasn't enough evidence of instability as
far as Ben was concerned. She'd been a fun person to trip with,
and acid seemed to have drawn none of the demons out of her
that it did, say, from Ben. He'd fought wars with screaming ban-
shees, with Wonder Woman riding him till he was pumped dry,
ululated the fact that his father had been a shepherd in another
life. He subscribed to *High Times* which took forever to crawl
and paddle its way down to Australia. He remembered bush
outings to Jarrahdale, Western Australia, when he was seven.
His father had revealed a death adder to him, curled up under a

78

log, its pointed head and fat body more alarming than poison, the great jarrah trees climbing with spiralling outbursts of bark into the Carnaby's cockatoo heavens. When it rained the water ran over granite and the outcrops and hills looked like they were crying. Disturbed in its winter sleep. He had never grown sophisticated enough to deploy it as a windfall, to capture the attention of potential partners. But it all came out tripping with Lucida, who said to him, You make me want to be an artist, Ben, you do you do you do. And what had he made of himself? – a hacker with the handle of Blitz. Blitz – why hadn't he gone with Death Adder or Tiger Snake, why hadn't he localised the global. They were his memories and then there was Lucida. She would plead not guilty. She had never believed in God's irony.

'The truth that is true for me'

IF ONLY I could be alone, thought Lucida in her cell, I could make art. She was in a secure unit, in her own cell, taking her exercise in the yard under supervision. She was on self-harm watch though had never raised a finger against herself. She loved repeating that to them, watching them fluctuate between serious-ness and laughter. Short-circuits them, she thought. She called up Duke, and he arrived begrudgingly. He hovered above the toilet. Like a guru, she said sarcastically. You're finding voice, he said. I sense Ben is trying to contact me, Duke . . . can you do something about it? I don't want any form of contact with him – I know he's gone into the service of the web. He is its slave. He is just another cracker, a white hat who thinks he is a black hat. All the black hats are white. They're all serving the God of Code. They're all its bitches. Holier than thou. Duke, I've been meaning to ask, did you like feathers? Why were you always bird-watching, searching them out? What do they have that I don't?

Lucida dismissed Duke and fell into a reverie. She was some-where. An island. There was volcano. There were pandanus trees. Black rock washed by the ocean. People were dancing on the rocks. It was evening, growing dark fast. There were bats. Lots of bats. And someone was flambeauing something on the beach . . . no, over a barbecue just off the beach while looking out into the purple-orange glimmer of where the sun had been. Had she ever been there? Lucida can't stand free-association. And now she's in a city, a small city on the island. There are platters of

prepared fruits being sold in stalls along a mall – a partial mall .
. . cabs are squeezing through or pushing people aside, people are
gathering outside the Agora, waiting for it to *open*. No. It doesn't
close over the lunch period. But shutters are up in other stores
and there are many arrivals at the mosque, the white of robes
and caps – kufis – glinting in the early afternoon sun. Grande
Mosquée. She asks someone in the crowd where she is. She is
speaking creole. She hears, 'Rue de Maréchal Leclerc walking
towards Rue Lucien Gasparin and the river flowing with mountain rain down to the ocean, fresh and salt water mingling along
the rocks in front of the Barachois, the cannons of the . . . French
East India Company . . . no . . . the Empire? She couldn't get a
fix on their period, so she thought she'd swing on down and take
a look, stopping for an ice confection at the Igloo on the way.

A woman of fashion propositions her. A zoreil outside the
Great Western where she has stopped to have a short black.
She stares into her cup and considers the offer . . . the request.
Blunt, to the point . . . Lucida likes that. It's so humid, even
inside in air-conditioning. Always damp. She delicately pops a
tear of sweat on her forehead. She says, Hmmm, maybe, but I
have to get to La Poste before it closes. Okay, I can walk with
you, insists the zoreil. Sure, why not – carpe diem and all that.
It's getting pretty windy. Oops, my skirt, sorry. I like it . . .
there's a cyclone . . . but it's not going to hit here . . . slipping
past to Madagascar. But we'll get some gales and a lot of rain.
Last year we got 1200mm in 12 hours and then rats poured out
of their hiding places and occupied all the schools desks around
the island. I was down here at the time – I visit this time every
year. Usually the cyclones have finished by now . . . this one is
late, as was last year's. But the weather's changing. Are you a sex
tourist? Lucida wanted to ask. But she didn't, and allowed herself
to be blown along by the circumstances. And somewhere, curled
up in air-conditioning or maybe in the cool of a cirque, maybe
somewhere above the plain of palms, curled up in the arms of
this stranger, her lover, she remembered passing a shrine of Saint
Expédit and knowing all the answers she wanted were here. No
one will spit at me here, she told herself. But then on the roads

driving down from Le Tampon an angry young man ran her off
an edge and into the waiting arms of post-Duke, always looking
so damned miserable. You can't keep taking it all for granted,
he told her. Histories of suffering won't allow for complacency.
You've always been too comfortable with your role. Your play.

She had never been culturally sensitive. In many ways, it was
a blank to her, peoples' differences . . . cultural practices . . . even
individual quirks. One of her teachers in primary school had said
to her parents, She's just very *individuated*. One of her pastels
had pride of place during open day (which struck Lucida as
odd given it was just after school) and all the parents filed past
cocked-eyed and disturbed, looking at the bloody red splotches
struck through with black lines. What is it? She refuses to give
it a title said her teacher, who wore Bali skirts and was very
'with it'. It's free expression. Is she an angry disturbed girl? the
minister's wife whispered to the teacher. No, she's very balanced.
She says she wants to grow up to be an arts reporter. What's
that? Oh, I think it's someone who interviews artists and writes
reviews of their shows. What an odd child and what an odd thing
to want to do with your life. An artist, well, I can almost understand
that . . . there are such beautiful paintings of faith in the world and
they are part of our appreciation of Christ, our Lord. But then
again, looking at this piece . . . don't you think it looks a little
disturbed . . . maybe she'd be better off being a female wrestler.
The minister's wife laughed at her own joke, so hard she let out
a little squeak of flatulence and said, Oops, sorry, and scurried
off to find her daughter who was playing outside with Lucida
and the others. No, Lucida had never been culturally sensitive
and couldn't understand why others ate different food from her
or wore different clothes or thought of their relationships with
the parents who provided those different clothes and foods as
being different from her own. Her parents were just facts. They
were ADULTS. What she ate and wore were just facts. She didn't
have much control over it. She didn't have much control over
what she wore and ate as a parent. But then, when she took
acid she had more control than most. Her brain didn't light
up. She didn't laugh much. She glanced through art exhibition

catalogues which she collected and marked with crosses when an artist particularly interested her. She was never interested in the works themselves, just the biographies of the artists.

*

But that wasn't Lucida's biography at all. She was born in Copenhagen (and Adelaide and maybe even Perth) and suffered heartbreak that few would survive. Duke reminded her of this, lost as she was in the deadzone of her cell. They're piecing this together, Lucida . . . your lawyers will paint a picture. Diminished responsibility. You should have them call me as a witness. Lucida ignored him. Lucida waved her hands through his ectoplasmic void. She denied him and went to the toilet, pulled down her trousers, hovered over the hole, and pissed into it with absolute indifference, absolute certainty.

Timeslip

I would have married if you'd had patience. Allowed paint to dry in the searing light of day, in the blast of cold at night. I would have made a new aesthetics of the past, of the days where tea-trees grow out of the city of Copenhagen, where that flimflam man, Ben, would be a dust mote in the attic, the attic where my precious documents will be lost and found. Some say that per Gods we are never in the right, but I know you think that's claptrap and that the only marriage is under the moon and the sun and in the eyes of the groundbirds you didn't think much of. But I implore, the cross of horizon and lone figure rising out of perspective is the true religion and we must approach its approach towards us. Your lustful predilections may or may not be a path, but it might also be the zimmer frame of ascension – so slow, so agonising for the snake to reach its own tail. So I say unto you, Lucida, let your interior grow and be born, and I will come down to you again and again. A family.

Sincerely,
Victor Eremita

Climacus Appears for the Prosecution

I CALL IT the incident of The Collection, he told them, piously. I knew punishment would come her way eventually. I was in the pew opposite, just across the aisle. The collection bowl was actually a velvet sleeve on a large wooden plate and people deposited their coins or pre-made-up envelopes into its mouth. The plate was passed from row to row and we children would usually excitedly if solemnly deposit the twenty or fifty cent piece our parents had given us. It was a middle-class congregation in a leafy suburb but it wasn't an historic church or anything. It was really more of a hall than a church – I mean, it was a church and all the High Anglican trappings were therein, but between services the pews were pulled alongside the walls and various events took place – plays were rehearsed, chairs placed in circles for discussion groups. Later a separate hall would be built like a T off the church and the pews stayed in their place. Yes, so I had a clear view of her when the plate was passed to her which she struggled with and almost dropped – it was customary for a parent to hold the plate so the child could slip the donation into the velvet sleeve but Lucida was headstrong, even if she rarely spoke above a whisper (which was extremely frustrating and the rest of us kids knew she did it to annoy), and grabbed the plate for herself. Then I saw her balance the plate on the back of the pew in front of her, slip her hand into the sleeve, and take out one of the envelopes. The envelopes would have the name of the donating family and would be part of an agreed upon weekly donation, usually five or ten or twenty dollars. I knew this because my father was very particular about how much was donated and wanted to ensure the money went to serving God and not the minister. I saw her take an envelope and somehow slip it into the front of her dress. It was a sleight of hand – almost magic. No one else noticed – it took a sharp-eyed child like me. I said nothing at the time, but I went up to her later that morning, after Sunday School (we'd been studying the story of Noah's Ark, I remember it all that clearly), and asked her what was in the envelope she'd 'borrowed.' Yes, I was being sarcastic – I was a smart even precocious child, I'll admit that. And she turned to me, bold as brass, and gently spat, Thin air . . .

The New Jerusalem

OUT ON A technicality, the newspapers said (back in the days before she had *complete* control). Others said, Avoids Prison and/ or a Secure Mental Health Facility. She escaped, slowly and leisurely, back to Western Australia. Out into the wheatbelt where towns were shrinking and the land was dying. Out to where they were offering free acreages on the edges of towns to attract 'population.' I will become culturally aware, she told one reporter, a young female arts reporter she'd agreed to speak with. Do you know the territory? the girl had asked. Of course not, Lucida had replied. Why would she bother going somewhere she already knew?

She didn't take up a free land offer, but settled on a small property of maybe ten acres out from a wheat bin town. She settled and kept settling. Her accounts had been frozen during the trial as there were claims her massive 'windfalls' from the sale of her shed/shack interiors, ghost images, and interior exteriors (those closing in mirage horizons) were both plagiarised and the result of co-opting Duke's many years of work. But with the technicality, this technicality had done its run. She had money and art supplies and a cement plank house surrounded by wandoos and not far from cropped paddocks.

Maybe she was an old woman by now, but it's not likely – she seemed to grow younger and younger by the day. Few knew who she was out there, but a man came with his small children and visited, staying in the nearest town's single motel of redbrick with a Spanish archway above reception. The kids complained that it was stinking hot and there was no swimming pool and that the old lady stank. It's the white spirits, the father said, and they spat back, Nah, she stinks of piss and returned to manipulating their gadgets.

Duke told her he could no longer see. He could just be there. I am fading, he said. I know, she replied. Can you tell me about the birds around here? Yes, she said, with the gentleness that had crept into her manner. How long has it been? he asked. Not long, she said . . . a few hours, days . . . minutes. You won't be in pain long, it will pass. She described a ring-necked parrot in painterly detail. She described a willy wagtail and its 'antics.' They call it a jiddy jiddy here, she said . . . I have been listening out. Learning? he wondered. Yes, maybe. She turned on the radio – only the ABC stations worked properly. She tuned into the classical station and she and Duke absorbed a few Scarlatti sonatas. I've paid too little attention to the nuances of sound in my life, she mused. Listen, he said, what's that birdcall? It was the 'hoo hoo' of the common bronzewing. Their wings glimmer bronze-green she told him. There's been a pair nesting in the wandoo just outside the kitchen window. I watch them when I make coffee.

The farmer who owns the five thousand acres next to these acres, my ten, wants to clear the bush that runs along our mutual fence – the bush on his side, on the other side of his firebreak. I protested when he came to tell me. Just being neighbourly, he said, with a thin, agonising grin. I'd rather you not, I told him . . . the birds and animals live in there. They fly from there to here. I watch them. Owls live in a hollow and at the top of the tallest tree which I think is a salmon gum there's an eagle's nest. They are a protected species, I added, as I have become aware, Duke, I have become aware. The farmer's grin went and he said, I was just being neighbourly, but if you want to play it that way. And now I know the bulldozer will come at night soon, come at night and knock it all down and he will pay whatever fine they ask and he won't care as the bush will be gone.

We can do something about it, says Duke. Maybe, maybe not . . . I am not sure if I have the energy left, Duke. You've worn me out. I've worn *you* out?

When I was a little girl my father told me off for drawing on the furniture. It was a lovely drawing, and I have changed my opinion about this. It was a drawing of a goat. He was angry and said, Not again. Then *I* drew a not-so-good drawing of a cow. His castigation had put me off and I was angry that he'd stifled my creativity. He took my pencils off me after the cow but I found out where he'd hidden them and retrieved them and drew all over his books and his study desk and the walls. I didn't draw anything in particular, I just drew. And you know what he did – for which I will forever hate him – he took the pencils back and snapped each and every one of them in front of me and dropped them in the bin and stormed off. I retrieved them and took the sticky tape from the kitchen drawer and stuck them all together and hid them under my bed. The next day he bought and offered me a new set, but I was having none of that. I took them and placed them in my cupboard and there they stayed until I left home. I have no idea what happened to them after that.

Duke's First Art Lesson

LUCIDA WASN'T INTERESTED in hearing Duke's story so he did his best to remember it to himself. The misty plaques were forming over his ghostly synapses, and things were growing confused and fading, but he doggedly worked at it until it came out. He spoke it to the open window, wondering about the filigree of leaves and branches that obscured the sun. It's like blackspots from looking into the flame of an arc welder, he thought.

My parents liked to party and by six years of age I was almost realising that I was more grown up than them. Or am I remembering someone else's parents. I don't know but I do know the first real art lesson I had was with my mother when she was tipsy after a party and seeing the babysitter off with a loud goodbye woke me and then saw me poking my face around the corner of my bedroom to see what was going on. I was still using a rubbery-plastic mushroom and forest animals nightlight which gave off a red and green glow, and that seeped out around me into the hall and gave it a sickly, scary feel. The nightlight that scares. Odd.

Mum says to me, Darling, what's wrong. Did I wake you … sorry! We were at a wonderful party tonight. Daddy is just taking the babysitter home. You like that babysitter? She seems like a nice girl. She's a teenager, I said. Yes, she is, Duke, yes she is. I can't sleep, Mum. What did you do at the party? It was in an art gallery, Duke … we looked at paintings and drank champagne and met the artist. What sort of paintings? I can't really, say, darling, she said, looking annoyed. Did the artist tell you about his paintings? Well . . . he didn't say much really . . . you should get back into bed before your father comes back and gets mad at you for being up so late. Really, you ask a lot of questions. What did the artist say, Mum? The nightlight shapes played on the makeup on Mother's face which was smudged and melting and I thought she looked like a clown . . . not a nasty clown, but a nice one. She was a nice, fun mum. Well, he said 'I prefer to let the paintings speak for themselves . . . ' and when she repeated this she lifted herself straight and made her shoulder square and spoke to the top of the doorframe. To tell the truth, darling, he was rather a pompous man but the champagne and canapés were first class. And then she crumpled a little – the alcohol was wearing off I realise now – and said, defeated, He said 'My paintings are about irony . . . look hard and you might see yourself reflected in them.' He sounds like a horrid man, I said, because I loved my mum and didn't want art or an artist to hurt her like this.

Loss of Speech

DID SHE CLEAN up under your feet?

They were long skirts she wore. Her shoes were clog-like.

Was the material pleasant to touch?

I was frightened of the monsters cast on the wall by the lace around her apron. When I was rolling around crying my eyes out, my brothers and sisters poking me with tridents, when I was down low and she was between me and the sun streaming in through the window, curtains pulled open and bunched together with sashes, I could see the monsters on the wall. It was a thin run of lace around the blank white slab of cotton.

I have noticed grotesque monster-like images in your many paintings of thin high clouds over desert, and especially in those of rare storms brewing over the dry salt lakes. Did they come out of that experience? Were you conscious of your mother's apron while you painted?

I never painted clouds, only monsters. I tried to tell her but no words came out of my mouth.

Is that why you never speak of her? Or have never spoken of her until recently?

There were no words.

Not even her name?

A name is a word. The dream of reason produces cities on red nights. It was Jutland that filled the space and I saw the fire eaters and dreamt of the dialectic of gold.

What is that?

Christ is a hero on the dry lake. He walks with a tragic gait.

This is a refrain?

This is a portrait of Lucida. This is the beginning of light on the page. This is the State of Origin, 1985. The case of Bigelow vs. Holmes. In three columns they marched out, dust at their tails. She was my Blue Screen of Death until she defaulted back to the sketch pad. I drew her genitals, disembodied, over and over. To make sense of the lacework, you see. Sometimes she just stepped over me and I looked up into the upside down canyon of dark. Nothing shone through those heavy skirts, though I could smell her even during those brief moments. A pleasant, musty smell. I salivated and then cried. I'd lost my zest – tuned out the cockatoos, the Sidney Nolan imagery, the desert community artworks spread out over the ground, built dot by dot. I'd lost it all in The Crash. It was 1845 and Rufus was getting the first four-pager *Scientific American* out . . . on the stands? *Industry and enterprise and other mechanical improvements. Patents (American). Improved rail-road cars. There is perhaps no mechanical subject, in which improvement has advanced so rapidly, within the last ten years, as that of railroad passenger cars. Let any person contrast the awkward and uncouth cars of '35 with the superbly splendid long cars now running on several of the eastern roads, and he will find it difficult to convey to a third party, a correct idea of the vast extent of improvement. Some of the most elegant cars of this class . . .*

Attraction is a curious power,
  That none can understand:
Its influence is every where –
  In water, air and land;
It keeps the earth compact and tight,
  As though strong bolts were through it;
And, what is more mysterious yet,
  It binds us mortals to it.

I always wondered if Lucida wrote that for Rufus. Notice the belief in God in science therein. Implicit but clear. I state this as recovery, I state this as the nacre, the chrism on her inside legs. I varnish the painting. I reframe. Eroded rock, so broken down. When the floods come the desert trees weep. White wash and wagtails skitting across our doubts. And then a tennis ball will float by, below the plimsoll line, heavy as it would have been in flight with the tattered bits of felt dragging it down. Just there, without a footnote. Orange sandstone offers a foothold for the low climb out – I hook my hands onto roo scats. Signs of fires gone up here – charcoal growth rings. Bullet shells – .303s. A dozen of them glinting in a heap – a cairn. Would you ask why? A desert monitor slow and fast at once, making shimmering Ss. This moonscape oasis, snake skin caught between lumps of quartz, sheoak nuts and needles but no trees. The crows do I Ching with these. And then a few succulents, the water approaching them filling far away, a mandala of lappings and bur-rowing marsupials that bounce small across the night. I suppressed the clumps of spinifex with her weight – a vulnerable, egg-bound night-parrot. Cats out here now. And wild camels. Residues and their home now, too. And then a town died – the nearest town, but still far away. Many mines closed. Gold. Japanese red light district on the outskirts. A dusty light of deliverance. Piles of desert oak and mallee used to fire the pumps, the water deep under the dry. It all soaks through as well as evaporates. This dry place is a water place, maybe more water than anything else. The sand is lace and the sky full of monsters eating any words that stray, that break free.

Lucida Sans

THE NEW YORK madman called it dowdy. Or was it shoddy? Or just 'poorly constructed.' Designed to be off-putting? The VD warning on public toilet seats? A font for every occasion, every mood. It was no relation.

He was a stick in the mud. And *even* a stick in the mud would be daubed over a canvas and called *innovative*. In his heart of hearts, he wanted to be able to perform his painting – a few strokes and the suggestion of an empire's downfall, all the moods of the madhouse. But these moments of light, these moments of classical I in my Sappho self, and all my Aphrodite disciples. Wings and smoke over the temple. An offering of my burnt flesh. The Duke of the Jukebox. Pub crawler. Gunslinger. Rolling up to entertain a Cambridge crowd, all scuffed boots and spurs, all gun-toting ecology. An edge effect hunter. A paradox waiver, a looper of acolytes, a fucker of Sleater-Kinney devotees. This is Lucida as it is, as she is, and it's not just sisterly spite or jealousy. I never wanted him. And his art was 1970s posters of horses galumphing across Marlboro Man territory. And his Namatjira phase was just a rip-off, and his 'Japanese Zen Phase' was second-hand paintings as haiku and brush strokes emptiness. Those minimalist poems. The time spent preparing a canvas, for toning up his 'students.' Phase-shift. Sei Shonagon. It's bloody cold in the desert at night in winter and that's good? And hot to the point of death in summer. And that's good? What possessed her? I'd bloody cut his throat if he made me feel like that. Possession. Boy's tricks. Those moonlit scenes, those screens she played our

childhoods out on. The court of the bedroom we shared, colour-
ing the same pictures, overcolouring each other. And then we'd
share a pillow, pulling our beds together, the single pillow bridg-
ing the two;-) Siamese twins. And our secret words written so
small, smaller than poems. But we had no magnifying glass. Our
lives will be sleep and love, we said. Sleep and love. Down to
the lower shrine. Firewood. A chrysanthemum. We celebrated
behind the screen of our room. She chased the first boy, not I.
She said to me, to me!, that he had 'Higher Qualities.' Her knees
glowed with worship. She dressed funny. She no longer wrote
me notes for the morning.

Schism: Was a Catholic Conversion in the Air?
Or Maybe a Departure from Christianity? Irony
in An 'Age of Terror' . . .

S/HE ARE ONE in their schism.

The Golden Age?

'KIERKEGAARD LED A somewhat uneventful life. He rarely left his hometown of Copenhagen, and travelled abroad only five times – four times to Berlin and once to Sweden. His prime recreational activities were attending the theatre, walking the streets of Copenhagen to chat with ordinary people, and taking brief carriage jaunts into the surrounding countryside.'[4]

I have nothing to do with either party. With neither part. What, seriously, does it mean to say, They gave it their all? Here am I, up on the top of a hill, looking out over hills, patching paintings together. The fact that I have *personally* only ever sold one painting (for $2300), is neither here nor there. I have given it my all. I paint without prejudice – I don't judge the farmer for killing the cow in the afternoon that I have painted in the morning. I find another cow, and adjust. There is no absolute, no perfect model. I came here speaking the language of the Church. I came here with all *censors* burning, with a notion to paint and repaint the view from a window. I found the window, I found the view, I painted. There is nothing lascivious in my work – I paint the cow, not the haunch of flesh bloody on the butcher's block. I familiarise myself with the people. I doorknock. Sometimes I am taken for a proselytiser, but nothing could be further from the truth. I have had many cups of tea, biscuits and beer. I am known as The Artist. I am no threat. I have made love with the blinds open and the sunset blazoning

4 William McDonald. Stanford Encyclopedia of Philosophy, "Søren Kierkegaard" (Winter 2017 Edition), Edward N. Zalta (ed.), https://plato.stanford.edu/archives/win2017/entries/kierkegaard/.

in but no one below or out on a neighbouring hill can see. I am
no traitor to my Church. I am no Abelard. I do not bring my
behaviours into my art. I am honest before my God. I am attuned
to the colouration of the place through listening to the red-capped
robin and the cycling calls of the ring-necked parrots. Their calls
splash colour about – a controlled frenzy. All in its place. Mine is
not to question. I do not have an opinion, not really, on the couple
(*any* couple) in question. I am outside art circles – that's what's
attractive about my work. I have left the Church but still believe.
The rituals remain. All that surety and energy behind me – all that
belief that art and spirituality are intertwined. To serve. To be honest, so much space . . . so many words, so much curatorial effort,
so much money . . . has been wasted on what amounts to a folly.
A Godless, murderous, debauched folly. We honest toilers . . . but
if you look closer, if you accept that the non-self-promoter such as
myself might have something to say . . . if you look, you will find
the answers. I am no show pony. No . . . no . . . I am proud to say
it is coincidence – Lucida has no connection by blood to me! We
are of very different families, with very different histories. There is
real art and there are lies. The self-serving and the serving. Reward
will come where it has been earned.

   I've bought a nice little second-hand car – nothing flash. And
get around the district. Go down to the IGA to do my shopping.
My wants are few. My art supplies come in via mail. I am on good
terms with the family who run the post office. They're from the old
Yugoslavia, you know. An older daughter has married a Christian
from *Borneo*. I don't go far – rarely down to the city. I visit the State
Gallery every now and again but it's a poor collection – whoever
does their local buying hasn't much idea. Gratuitous. Lot of apo-
logia for being here stuff. Can't say much about it, of course. Have
them up in arms. The locals know about it. Some have asked me
to paint it. I tell them, my art isn't political – what kind of real art
is? But if you look hard at the paddocks and farmhouses and trees
lining driveways – deciduous, splendid in Autumn – you might read
something in. Not that we should. A painting is just a painting. It
should make us feel good. Good about the world. About ourselves!

Much later it is learned that Thomas David was really . . . and that The Duke was present at his historic speech advocating the Uranium Project which was destined for government approval . . .

HE WROTE HIS report of the 'expedition' under the name of Thomas David (or Vigilius Haufniensis in the Old Tongue). He wrote as an 'impartial observer' of himself. He published the piece in a well-respected online newspaper. He accounted for his sins and called himself (also) 'Watchman of the Harbour.' He admitted to sourcing art supplies from factories known to indulge child labour.

Uranium was the game. The environmental approvals were pretty well sewn up but he felt he should personally speak to the traditional owners. After all, the company bore his name. The land they were mining was part of his father's massive pastoral lease. He had known many of the people since he was a child. He was addressing those of the community who were on-side, who understood the material wealth and jobs his company would bring them. His people had orchestrated a shut-out of the opposition, those of the people affected by greenie propaganda, those who had it all wrong. But in his report he played it neutral. Stick to it being Duke himself – don't muddy the waters further. Ha!

We know a little about what happened in the meeting because The Duke (alias Thomas David) had travelled from the lake's edge and stood at the back of the hall. It was a long journey, but still local. He consulted with a couple of community artists from both sides of the divide. It is known that as a child, The Duke had been exposed to a significant dose of radiation. A piece of enriched yellowcake that was given to him as a curio. He said that it affected his fertility, his libido, and brought a recurrent listlessness. He precluded himself from life insurance on the basis of it. There is television footage of him protesting against nuclear warships in various Australian ports, but it is not known if he was there to oppose nuclear energy per se or American militarism or both of these factors.

In the interview he mentions *watching* Thomas David at work – trying to work an audience who knew exactly who he was, what he was and how far his largesse extended. (The) Duke swore there was no alter ego involved. Thomas David is real, he insisted – a separate Aussie entity. A sentient being. He is ageing separate from me.

On their own lands, the people knew he wanted to be brother and big white father at once. He spoke to the elders as if they were country cousins, to the young people as if they needed to pull their noses out of the petrol tins and get a real job. He spoke of solving the world's energy needs, of the people retaining their identity and contributing to the well-being of the planet. When an infiltrator – leader of the opposing group within the community – called out that Chernobyl and Fukushima were the future if such projects went ahead, that all the company wanted to do was profit from the planet's last gasps – he was shouted down by the great white prophet. Via Thomas David, The Duke was offered a vast commission to furnish the Big Bull Uranium Company's offices in Perth with art for the workers. Thomas David mentioned that the artist had been *present* as if it were a validation. The fact that The Duke told him to stuff his commission was not mentioned. Artists from the community were tapped for paintings – offers were made *they couldn't refuse*.[5] The Big White also said to the artists – you don't have to live without proper plumbing, without amenities. And he talked over hunting trips out on the boundaries of the station. He used the words 'dreamtime' and 'walkabout' and called two elders by their traditional names. He wore a magnificently casual non-intrusive set of jeans, shirt and boots. The artist mentioned these and their brand names in the interview. The camp dogs were kicked by publicity people. Four-wheel drives drove a dozen company people away around sunset for the dangerous drive to the nearest town (four hours) through 'roo country.'

---

5 Many did refuse . . .

When Lucida had briefly moonlighted as a theatre critic and had encountered 'Thomas David' at His Majesty's in Perth. When was this? Years back. A career path not (really) pursued.

You are reviewing this play for which newspaper?

Ah, a serious publication. Don't mention you saw me here. [His lips oscillate in & out, in & out, like he's consuming himself. Gobbling himself up. Yum. Magnificent.]

I won't. I am reviewing the play, not the audience. [She is moving the tip of her left shoe in a dainty circle in front of her. He is fixating.]

You have a strong face. You are an intelligent woman. I am establishing research positions in the arts at a variety of universities. We have a lot to thank mining for. [His face reddens as he tosses off his glass of white wine.]

I have to go to my seat, the bell has tinkled. [She manages to place, precisely, a drop of moisture on her top lip just below the philtrum.]

I will look down at you and smile. You know SHE wouldn't be here without support from my foundation. [Even Lucida is shocked with how blatant, how grandstanding he can be. She worries he might spontaneously combust and stops moving her shoe and steps back slightly.]

Yes, I know. You have been a boon for arts in this State. Where would they be without you. [She doesn't bother with sarcasm – what's the point?]

Let's catch up after the show. I will introduce you to my wife *and* the director. The director is heading to New York after this show to catch some gems. That's a lovely red you're wearing. [It is a lovely red, and she will say so. She loathes the director and the director loathes her. As for the wife – who knows?]

Yes, I know. Red is my colour.

[Lucida registers the ladder in her stocking and jokes, Oh, well, that's one ladder to Paradise you won't be climbing, buster!]

Postscript: Did Lucida and (The) Duke's Sighting of a Night Parrot Elicit Sweet Nothing from Either at the Salient Moment?

DEATH WISH. REDUCED to symbol. Obsessive implosion of latter-day explorer syndrome. Proof. Cats and foxes. Specimen in a wire fence. We get dragged into the moment, into the rapid flit to water. Dusk stuff. But it wasn't one night parrot, it was a dozen. And not the Bourke's Parrot variety. In her only moment of weakness, Lucida confessed to Duke as his breath was expunged over the expanse, filling it with pioneering heritage, with residues of the between-the-wars Euro avant-garde, with noises like clucks and purrs that might have been a vocal-cord sonata, she confessed that she often thought her soul was that of a transmigrated night parrot. That she dug in her dreams into sandy burrows beneath spinifex tussocks, that she could feel the fully formed eggs inside her waiting to be laid. She said, This is no battery hen trope. This is no aspiration. This is no correlation or collusion or drawing together of colonial ambiguity – a linguist's tapping into, a living vicariously through feather and beak, through seed nubbed from the desert floor. And Duke, pop-eyed, seeing it all in his suffocation, saw that she was true to her word. Saw that she was the essence of the artist. Saw all his retreats and refinement of craft. He wanted to say, Craft is all that matters. Craft is in the artefacts I leave behind. He cast the representation, the advocacy of the obscene Thomas David aside, and winged it – went it alone.

My name will be as great as the few nineteenth-century

specimens of night parrots. And the most recent fallen. Craft is mine name. I have sold out to ambiguity, to slippage. Irony has replaced the sincerity of the endangered bird we all want to identify with. And so Lucida eased his going. In reconstruction after reconstruction, in installation on installation, she is sucking his O so precious lifeforce in order to have her time, to be the woman artist escaped from the imprisoning Biblical story. She yelled Isaiah – all of Isaiah – at the top of her voice. She made a yodel that echoed as if they were amidst high mountains. Her gender despair, her personal variation on *Fortvivlelse* knew no boundaries. She lapped up the Socratic. She yodelled and yodelled and beneath her The Duke, fully evacuated, smiled. Night parrot – 'Eiron' – flocked and flocked and was bountiful. Unwanted in its profusion, the night parrot opened the lake road to a higher grade of uranium – maybe even 20 or 25 g/t. Centipedes crawled from Duke's nostrils and Lucida proclaimed Surrealism had finally belatedly arrived in Centralia. She had become epic, she had become mythical, she had become hideously beautiful. She was beyond taxidermy.

The First End.

The Second Coming of Ben: An Echo of an Earlier Ignored and/or Forgotten Manifestation

BEN WENT AS far away as possible. As far away from the uniden-
tified subject. He walked and walked until his feet could walk no
further. They had become ill feet. He rested up. He read Deleuze
and Guattari and subjected himself to Schizopsychiatry. He sent
hand-written letters to old friends and they all complained back
via email that there was no sense of place in his missives outside the stamps on the envelope and the postmarks which were
smudged anyway. If you're 'over there' we at least want a sense
of *it* – the place itself, the resonance and particularities of 'it'
itself – we want to feel part of us is there. Some of them were
drifting further away from him anyway, especially in the light of
his newly acquired retro view of the world. He grew no beard, he
wouldn't play Ingress, and said portals were just a fancy name for
portaloos. He now considered himself an artist, having stepped
into the shoes of the lost one. Makes it worse, they said. It does.
It. Of all people, still lusting after the Lucida via the ghost of
Duke as magnified in Lucida, you need an augmented reality,
and with all that walking walking walking, why not make it work
for you and us at once. Exergame!

But truth be, laid up in his room which looked much like
rooms elsewhere, the blinds drawn and codeine phosphate
his security and bedfellow, he imagined himself in the wheaty
regions of Western Australia, striding past a paddock just as an
old bastard shot a neighbour's dog and then his own dog because
it came sniffing around. He was wandering with the mental

image of Lucida who told him, I will make of this an installation, a happening. I will walk naked through the stubble and dead dogs will float like planets obliterated during a galactic war. Ben could see this, he could, and he scratched at his genitals, which had that slow unscratchable itch he hated and loved a little.

He thought to himself and he thought to Lucida, Surely art is here and yesterday, surely it is a scratchy holding the prize-winning symbols imminent beneath the silvery plastic. I rub away the layers, brass art. Lucida would whisper, I walk the silvery water across the meniscus of bogs, I stuff my wounds with bog cotton, I turn to wisps when the furze burns along the mountain ridges, I shelter under hawthorn trees in full bloom. Does it matter where I am? I paint in my ectoplasm and the Church cannot touch me. I am Ireland, I am Denmark, I am Borneo, I am England, I am Australia. I am the colonial subject.

Ben had told no one of the migratory flight, in itself weeks too early. Out-of-kilter seasons. The paint wouldn't adhere to the rough seas and the desert followed in the wake. The bleached reefs and the bleached anuses and the sceptics high on their Virgin clouds.

Lucida, I try hard not to be a smart arse, I try hard not to narrativise. I try hard not to be a try hard. I have located you in myself. I am going to have the wound lanced and you will be cut out.

The New Ben Decides He Will Write a Lightly Fictionalised Story of Lucida's Relationship with (The) Duke

SELFISHNESS IS AN asset when you're dying of thirst. Did either of them say this, breaking the constraints of gender? Binary was the art form they shared. A description of budgies drinking at the edge of a large puddle formed by a freakish rain event in Centralia does double duty – it tells us much about the vulnerable love of Duke for the idea of Lucida, of Lucida for Lucida. Set thirty years earlier than it happened, allows for room to manoeuvre. Levity is the luxury of long-lost brand names or incipient familiarity. Authentication.

Little is known about the series they conjured together, based (loosely) on Blake's 'Red Dragon Series.' It might be conjectured that they were based on an actual sighting. It was during Duke's 'it has to have really happened in order to paint it' period, and Lucida was up for anything. She just wanted to 'be there.' But it would be fair to say that if Duke got them happening, it was Lucida who gave them their fire.

Lucida: Australia is a land of reptiles.

Duke: And fire. Always fire but also *increasingly* fire. Increasing fire. [This is an interpolation or maybe a harbinger of climate change or maybe just early realisation: it was a particularly hot period in the region . . .]

Lucida: I love the scales of its belly.

Duke: They aren't (remotely) vulnerable.

Lucida: They are Emu Plains and Woomera.

Duke: Houston, we have a problem.

Lucida: At Her Majesty's . . .

Duke: Request.

Lucida: The colonisation of wheat.

Duke: No wheat will grow out here.

Lucida: Then why do *they* clear the spinifex?

They nicknamed their first red dragon 'Thomas' for no particular reason. Thomas is hungry this morning. Thomas is angry this morning: a dry lightning storm is brewing. Thomas is parched. They labelled to negate. That red dragon lost its power over them but the others that followed were nameless and grew and grew. The series, as a consequence, had to be destroyed. Tarkovsky tormented and murdered that horse. How to make art without teeth. And without mythology. And sewing dragons' teeth to make armies. How to have action without weapons. Neglect is a violent act. They knew all this, waking and painting and inhaling the chemicals of their trade. They watched dragons fly long after their destruction and the haunted were haunted. These ghost stories without houses to settle in, to possess. No amount of protest will bring the visions under control. Real as real can be. Backwards and forwards. What's the diff? Seriously, what's the split differential where the wheels can get no traction anyway? Sand zone. And so they settled to watch *Mouchette* by Robert Bresson, and grew sick with its cruelty, its animal abuse. The switch-off function in their shared headspace was broken. There were narrative consequences. This is what art historians might call the End of the Honeymoon Period.

Addiction: *Opbyggelige Taler*

SHOW DON'T TELL. Anglepoise lampoon. Going back and forth and waiting. Sitting outside strange houses in strange suburbs in old cars, waiting. And then getting and being disappointed and angry and waiting. Hungry and hungry and then sometimes sick with surprise. That's how you fall.

What tendencies in childhood? For Lucida, she remembers being sick to the stomach at the thought of the ghost train but compulsively going back to it. She spent all her show money (and that was plenty) indirectly on being groped by teenage boys and vomiting afterwards. Duke had a thing for fairy floss. He ate it till he vomited. Hated it but couldn't get enough. Easier to paint spew than describe it.

Lucida spoke to her first police officer when lost at her first Royal Show. A crowd of thirty thousand and she lost, with her plastic pinwheel poking up not quite flaglike, and the propellers spinning with the hyped-up breath of teenagers. A mauve-headed woman guided her to the police booth and an announcement went out. She was crying but liked hearing her name called out over the speakers. When asked her name she didn't hang on to it but said it fifty times without pause. Lucidalucidalucidalucidalucida lucidalucidalucidalucidalucida-lucidalucidalucidalucidalucidalucidalucidalucidalucidalucidalu-cidalucidalucidalucidalucidalucidalucidalucidalucidalucidalucid-alucidalucidalucidalucidalucidalucidalucidalucidalucidalucidalu-cidalucidalucidalucidalucidalucidalucidalucida! She had a spangly star on her top and the police officer described that in

111

detail and her height and her weight (approx) and the colour of her hair. She was wearing pointy red shoes but the police officer never referred to them. Lucida couldn't tell or wasn't interested in whether or not the officer was male or female. She was indifferent to whether or not her parents or whoever was actually looking after her, found her. She wanted to go to the toilet but held on and thought she would burst.

Lucida's Reconfiguring of Duke's Life (With Her)

DUKE SAID THE wrong things at school and got the cane. He was telling the story and then he was driving in the northern Western Australian wheatbelt. He was near Morawa, he'd been looking at the stone of the Hawes Church, then there was a dead kangaroo on the road and a large wedge-tailed eagle perched on its distended belly, and then he was further down the road and standing on the shoulder, studying a wreath flower. That is more perfect than death, he'd said, and sketched it on the back of his hand. A tattoo that no others would see after a few days, but he'd see always, like the marks of the cuts from school.

That was school in Western Australia. He told Lucida he'd also been to school in Ireland and England and America. He was verbally abused in those countries, but not physically attacked. Though in America he'd seen a non-believer branded by a Christian teacher with the word, *Believe*. A hot iron, an iron heated by a cigarette lighter. A public school, not a Christian school (as such).

And Duke surprised Lucida once by adding that he'd spent a few months in an English-language international school in Copenhagen. It was near a fairground in the middle of the city, he added. There was a cinema nearby. I was a boy for all seasons, he told her. She cried. She cried tears of red dust. That happened around the time the Green Candidate drove out to them in the shack and said, Vote 1 ME. He was armed to the teeth. I like shooting vermin, he said. It helps the environment. Duke told him to piss off, but the Green Guy thought he could cadge on to Lucida and tried to impress her with his big weapon. You're just a greenhorn, she flirted, knowing that the wild birds would pick the ruby sleepers from his earlobes before he made it back to his sparkling four-wheel drive. At least I don't claim to have morals, she said to a stricken Duke later that night. And, what's more, she added, he should have known better than to take on the crows with that prosthesis of his. There's something twisted inside of you, said Duke, when he managed to lift himself from the powdery sack of his bed. Lucida was wearing the ruby sleepers like trophies. What you fail to see, said Duke, is that he will go back to Head Office and be lauded and acclaimed. They'll call him a real bushy and even the Hunters and Fishers party followers will abandon their hero and flock to the Green Party in droves. He is the New Green Hero – he is the prophet who will now guide them out of the wilderness. And, what's more, he will attract the protest vote. You have aided and abetted the enemy.

In an angry moment, Lucida told Duke the true history of Arthur Boyd's Nebuchadnezzar paintings. Have you read Max Weber, she asked him? Do you know the palette stolen from the cows of the sun? Duke did, but played dumb. Then, Lucida said, It came down to successful shows in London and New York, only then was Australia validated. It's an issue that goes way back. Duke had a distant relative who'd been a minor player in the Heidelberg School and Duke'd inherited a small European landscape which he used as a beer coaster. It has stood up remarkably well to much wear and tear, though he had had the small canvas embedded in Perspex (which had yellowing stress lines through it). It went from France to Copenhagen to Australia where it doesn't look the same. But some famous Australian works painted in the appropriate locale or vicinity were clearly influenced by it. Sidney Dickinson wanted to latch on to something. Lucida insisted that mob had no idea about the outdoors and the bush was backlit and they couldn't see the wood for the trees which were chopped down anyway. Not that she disapproved, being ecologically retrograde herself, but she detested the *act* of *painting*. She preferred, instead, the act of acting painting. Further, the idea of an exhibition of paintings as opposed to an exhibition for an exhibition's sake, disturbed her. What do you mean by that? asked Duke. It makes no sense, he mumbled, the night parrot burrowed so deep into his brain that he was as much bird as human. He could, however, fly higher and further than the night parrot. He had great hopes for survival, not yet fully understanding precisely what it was Lucida was a harbinger of. Flies and midgies were stuck in the swirled paint of the palette. Duke cried over the suffering and death. He would have thrown the mixings away but Lucida insisted this reality would lift his art to greatness. Looking into the heat signature, mirages crossed over to make skyscrapers over the salt flats with tunnels and crossroads. In those chiasmuses . . . chiasmi . . . he found his light and dark and lit a plethora of inner truths. The paintings looked beaky. He dropped the lid of the Prussian Blue tube into the vortex of the canvas and started to shake with vision. He was drowning and yelling, Calenture, calenture, calenture . . . like there was no tomorrow, like all land deeds had been stripped away and a gradual returning was taking place before his very eyes. It was true, he wanted the best of both worlds. But he didn't want to share it outside the community that knew of his presence, that was appalled by his quoting Patrick White's *Voss* as some kind of white truism. You're speaking bullshit, said Duke, blunt as blunt can be.

I wish to exhibit God, said Lucida with a rush of blood. There is *it* and *God*. I am it. She quoted a line from a Crass song she'd heard when going out with a friend of Ben's, Hendy. Hendy was a punk who went from Perth to London to join the Crass commune. He found Penny Rimbaud in a run-down old house out in the country boiling up a pot of split peas. Hendy pitched his one-person tent which even out there was still a one-man tent, and listened to the meadows aestivating. *In all your decadence . . .* that's how Hendy began every diatribe against Perth and its mining-boom materialism. Why was Lucida even there, in the Stoned Crow Winehouse, drinking Kirup Syrup with Hendy and listening to British Migrants trying to make punk happen all over again? Hendy's mohawk was green and he didn't call himself a punk. He was an anarchist: *Punk is Dead,* he said or quoted. For a while, he ran a punk that's not punk programme on the university station RTM. He propelled an old-fashioned scooter along Stirling Highway to work long before scooters were bladed and fashion. Hendy hated fashion. The wheels kept falling off his scooter.

What is studio to you? asked Lucida when she was still an arts journalist who wasn't. Between bouts of dry vomiting, and while banging the corrugated iron walls with a stick, kicking up a hell of a beat, Duke did his best to answer. He was lucid and sincere, despite everything. Everything.

Studio is contact. It lays no claims to legitimacy.

I have a reminiscence I want to share, Duke had said to Lucida. But let's take it into the present without mediation. Duke says. He is saying it now. No tricks.

I remember driving a narrow hedged road high into the Caha mountains crossing over into Kerry from West Cork. My aim was to go above the snowline. Sheep raddled red on the road, which was wide enough for one car. If another approached, it was a long dangerous reverse up or down.

Were you scared?

Scared is not the right word. With light snow falling I could see enough to imprint for studio purposes. I would take *plein air* to the cleaners, soak out the sheep shit stains, size the canvas in snow.

Snow is overrated.

There is going to be less and less snow. Snow will come in storms and drown us or not at all. It will be an issues of tenses.

How do you transfer tense to a canvas?

By being where you were all over again. Bringing the outdoors indoors.

Gallery.

Gallery is never indoors. That's imprisonment.

Gallery as prison?

Maybe. I did an interview once with a young man from the university. He wouldn't take no as an answer. He forced his way into my hotel room by stealing the maid's magnetic room card. A skeleton key card. I was in bed, sick. I answered and groaned and demanded he leave which he wouldn't. I stuck my arse out of

bed at him, the two eyes you know on my arse cheeks glowering at him. He told me I flattered myself. And he laughed.

Which hotel was it?

Does it matter?

Of course.

It was the Hilton in Melbourne.

I had sex with ten strangers in a room in the Hilton in Melbourne. A marathon session which my then girlfriend videoed. An installation. It was before I was an artist. Before you made me.

I don't like that laugh of yours Lucida.

No, Ben used to say it was 'unbecoming of me.' Hysterical in the context, no?

You're tedious.

I think gossip and nasty talk is the spice of life, Duke. You should get with the programme.

I don't need words.

But your paintings are full of words, Duke. Hey, here's some fun facts about my life. I have Huguenot heritage – my great great great great grandfather was a weaver who went from the Sussex countryside to London and became a barber. His father and mother came over from the Continent – escaped, you know – and had to sign everything with an X. X was the European script – universal within its confines. The paradoxical chiasmus of identity. My great-grandfather visited the Soviet Union and said that seeing the embalmed corpse of Lenin was the highlight of his life. And another fun fact: I smeared part two of my first period over my bedroom walls and signed it with an X.

Lucida, can't you leave me alone. I am tired. I will go for a walk along the track. I will pray.

Pray to what?

To the failure of light.

You're such a jerk, Duke.

With Duke out of the picture for a while, Lucida undressed and stood in the doorway (such as it was), looking out, occasionally stroking her desert patina skin. She wondered how she might get through to Duke. Nothing seemed to disturb him massively though everything seemed to disturb him more than a little. She became pensive and misty and vague and inhabited an earlier skin when she'd been 'feral' and encamped with a group of other young protestors in the jarrah forests of Western Australia. She had been designated the camp artist, and she scratched lovehearts and arrows and letters into the loggers' machinery at night. Soon the forest would be gone and all the shits she'd done behind old growth trees would be squashed by *TIMBER* or by the big boots of the loggers. There wasn't a female logger among them. No female boots would be treading in her shits, though a few of the barefooted girls from camp had squished her mists through their toes over the weeks. One always giggled when such things happened. But shitting in the forest under the roosting Carnaby's cockatoos and amongst the last of the mainland quokkas in that neck of the woods was a joy in itself, the stars penetrating the canopy and beatifying every defecation. Now, that was prayer, robust and purposeful. And she'd been so stoned on the last of the dope plants harvested before downfall, that it was embedded. Spiking the tanks of dozers with sugar was part of the beauty, but it wasn't the only beauty. Lucida knew herself part of the images and texts of the universe, and melded as she released her nutrient waste to the vulnerable, soon-to-be-dead forest.

El Niño was Lucida's placebo. She loved it as she loved herself. Once, diving among the Great Barrier reef's dead corals . . .

Land Art: Lucida Defines 'Home' When Challenged by an Ex of Duke's [and wherein the worth of coffee table art books is debated]

Duke's desert dry salt-like spiral was inspired by me! the Ex claimed, much to Lucida's chagrin.

I was there, she snapped back. And I can tell you, I was omnipresent.

Well, I've been told you were there *after* the fact, Lucida. You might have witnessed it post its making, and you might well have been the photographer who recorded it – might well – but as for inspiring it? Well . . .

Lucida's back arched. She felt catlike. She was ready to pounce. Duke wanted to outdo Smithson because he knew I wouldn't be satisfied with imitation. Duke knew my desires before I arrived. He longed for my arrival. It was his gift to me. No tribute to a master, but an acknowledgement of his need for me to arrive, to be there. It was the interview he had to have, and I was the interviewer he had to have. Lucida enjoyed being bitchy. It was inevitable she'd have to deal with these wannabes – book launches are golden opportunities for smiling putdowns. And the launch of Lucida's *Duke: His Inspirations*, was a magnet to the bitter, jealous and maladjusted. Lucida forgot about the Ex though the Ex's mouth went up and down and round and round. Lucida was thinking over her thank-you speech and contemplating whether or not to let the CEO of the mining company . . . that had so kindly underwritten the cost of this very very expensive coffee table book in the name of Australian

Art and The Future. He was a very mature man, but he spruced
up well and the 'snow on his temples' reminded him of ancient
classical Chinese poets. *They* knew how to make love, she was
sure. She was certain.

*

The spiral into the salt lake brought the rain. Duke was sure of
this. The dry had to come to an end and the pink gypsum was
shining loud enough to attract the Big Australian to the location.
It was a small spiral – no earth moving equipment had been
used in its making. Rather, he'd dug into the lake bed by hand,
and made a gentle mound in a spiral shape, capped off with the
strange shells – so small – that littered the fluxive edges of the
lake. Snail shells? What were they, bleached so white, spirals in
themselves? And it was this Lucida confronted and took on as
her own. Duke, she said, I am going to use the magic of my
digital camera to change the scale of this. To the world, it will
look massive. But, Lucida, I don't want the world thinking I've
damaged the land. It's art, Duke, art . . . clearly you've never
really understood your own calling. All else is expedient. We do
it for their own good. It looks like a Neapolitan birthday cake,
she said. That's the shells and the salt and the gypsum and the
blackness underneath turned out to the light. It's like rock but I
find it works like sand in my hands. Some of it is sand, he added,
but mostly it's like rock.

*

Inside the gallery. Around a model of the salt like spiral, cham-
pers was quaffed. The Workshop of Lucida had put the scale
model together. It was close to the proportions of the original,
but who was to tell. A young woman played an electric violin
at the centre of the spiral. Setting up, Lucida had taken the
risk and touched the violinist in a rough-gentle way on her left
breast. The Workshop took a risk and giggled, knowing Lucida
was sure to have her way. But then, the workshop was entirely
made up of young men with hipster beards – not one of them

older than twenty-six. Twenty-six is the death of youth, Lucida says, and you will have nothing to give me when you expire. The 'boys' called Lucida 'The Vampire' behind her back, but she was pleased when whispers of this reached her. Typical, she laughed. She was good in her own company.

But Lucida knew she wasn't really like this. It's all just for show, she said to herself. She had a role to play and she'd play it because revolutions happen out of view, behind the obvious. And if anything, Lucida was a revolutionary. She was ready to move on to the next phase of her programme.

Duke had said, These are dingo tracks, Lucida – see they are close to the kangaroos' track. A doe and her joey just out of the pouch. The doe is injured – see the dark taps of blood on the dust. Lucida assumed Duke was giving another of his interminable grasshopper art lessons, another dose of sagacious benevolence, and she said, humbly, The earth is our canvas of life (Master). Don't be daft, girl, he said, It's nothing to do with art!

She sold a hundred books at the launch. Each book signed with a flourish, a curlicue. It's not a time to be understated. She told herself. On the cover, a close up of Duke's left nipple encrusted with grey hair. There he'd been, standing out in the sun in a pair of khaki shorts and thongs and a panama hat, looking like a wally, and she'd snapped him up. The left nipple was the best bit. He could be such a dickhead. A man who sold real estate and who'd bought four copies of the book asked her to autograph his forehead. He was so pissed and his wife was cringing with shame – the perfect moment. She signed and the swish at the end of the signature took black permanent marker directly onto his eyeball. He barely winced. Then there was the mining CEO who offered to buy the spiral replica for the foyer of his company's new skyscraper in St George's Terrace, Perth. The Fremantle Doctor rips in along there, he said, and does a Marilyn Monroe to even the most PC young woman's dress, he said, slightly tiddly. Then sensing reporters nearby, he struggled . . . Not that young women *wear* dresses now. No. I mean, they wear what they want. Lucida saved him with her compassion, Yes, I've heard that old chestnut before, darl . . . from the days of, what was it,

The Weld Club. You're so witty dredging it up and giving it new life. He looked at her bemused but grateful. He wondered why all his PR training and gender workshops had run out the door in a moment of hysteria. It's fucking art, Lucida would discover (too late?) that he was thinking, dedicating himself to bedding the artist or whatever she was within the week.

*

Lucida is looking truly glam by this stage. She is doing guest segments on an ABC late night arts television programme. And then she's in makeup and discovers Duke's Ex is appearing on an episode with her. Why wasn't I told? she yelled under the blush. Told what? asked the makeup artist who had not taken to Lucida though admitted she had nice skin. That the Ex – bitch! – was going to be on the show! Lucida had moved on from launch mode and was in the attack zone. Beethoven's Second Piano Concerto was being piped over the speakers, agitating her more and more.

Across the curve of the panel Lucida gave disguised daggers eyes to the Ex, who was rambling on about her early years with Duke. God almighty! she was on the fucking programme to talk about the Degas exhibition at the National Gallery, not rave about Duke's Sufi Stage. Good *on pointe*, nice ballet shoes . . . Lucida interrupted, politely, I think we're getting off topic. The dancers . . . But the host was running with it and there was no stopping the Ex with her boosted breasts and pinched back ears and lashings of raven hair dye. The vanity of that woman, thought Lucida, who turned her attention to the young poet next to her who was starring at calluses on his hands as if surprised at how they'd got there. And then mid the Ex's next sentence, Lucida interrupted again, and said, I think our poet here made an interesting point about the correlation between Degas and Baudelaire . . . I think it's important we can consider Degas outside his influence on . . . and then she blew it . . . fucking Australian fucking art. That'll be edited out, she added, and with a smirk from the poet she went hammer and tong(ue)s, grabbed the poet's hands, and said, Now what the fuck are musical hands like this doing with calluses and blisters all over them. The poet said, You know when a great old York gum is going to lose a limb to termites and strong easterlies when lots of saplings appear not far from its base, it's done its time. Precisely, said Lucida, as the host said, Steady on everyone, come on . . . we've got a show to record. And then the Ex sealed the deal, The fucking poet has calluses from masturbating too much. He's just another wanker. Like you, Lucida, like you. You're a wanker. A fucking blokey wanker. And with this, Lucida snotted her and took the consequences.

*

Settled out of court. A handsome sum is a status symbol. That's art, Koons, that's art. Lucida selected Spiderbait's *Greatest Hits* and sang 'Black Betty' to herself as she steepled her way through Martin Place.

*

The mining CEO actually wore silk boxers and garters. I would paint you if I could, thought Lucida, then took heart that Tracey Emin had been made a drawing professor in London. She turned the whale on his stomach with a hand and a fist, and sat on his legs, singing Yoko Ono screaming opera style and he told her his pole – he actually said *pole* – was hurting it was so inflamed and sticking into the mattress. Lucida opened her fist and uncapped a minibar bottle of Bourbon, hoicked the silken boxers down and inserted the neck of the bottle into his rectum. That'll give you a blast! What are you doing? he yelped, trying to buck her off his back, finding she was stronger than she looked. Fucking installation art, you cunt. Lap it up. Love it. You are a piece of fucking art. It's the age of the miner, Calloo-callay, no work today!

*

Coffee table books. Remember that episode of *Seinfeld*, the *Old* Ben (her Ben, the *real* Ben) had said, Where the coffee table and the coffee table book became one and the same. Lucida had cut him off short. She'd drawn her straw and was sticking with it.

She had little time for raw unadulterated popular culture at the time, being less kinetic than at present. Do you think I paint a sympathetic self-portrait? she asked the Old Ben, who she didn't recognise. Just another admirer, a cipher to absorb her chat. Or maybe he was an arts journalist? Yes, likely. She would continue chattering away. What's your name? she asks eventually. Ben, he says, wanting to be recognised. But nothing. She doesn't see *her* Ben, she sees a stranger. Strange name, Lucida says after a pause . . . You don't hear that name much these days. You know, verbally speaking, she added. I mean, if I am being forward, and tell you I know of Duke before I meet him, this backwards me encountering my destiny, my faith, by joy and misery, would it displace me in your affections. You are my scaffolding of the present, Old Ben. I have a good feeling about you in the here and now. NOW I rely on you. Just for the moment. But you know . . . ships in the night and all that. Sorry, but I am just SO ME. I am a female Faust. I am so. And so, you pirates laugh at me! No, not you Old Ben, faithful lapdog, true companion. This is my ethical phase, Old Ben. I make decisions on this basis. The consequences of my actions. O telos Duke. Duke to be. Company. Old Ben was shattered when she went (back to) her own way, forgetting even to say goodbye. I never ever existed for her, he cried. Wounded. Mortally wounded.

*

Crime. The beneficiaries. Plain as day. A schooldays story, New Ben – angry, vengeful. Bitterness has twisted his features. Lend me an ear. An exquisite pleasure that cost me. It all changed on that May Day when Daddy told me one of us was the child of the cleaning lady. A young woman who'd come to the house to clean and he'd been taking a shower and heard the knock and let her into the corridor with his towel around his waist and the bathroom door open and steam spilling out and he joked, Clean in here first.

*

Lucida becoming Duke was evident early and there was no deny-
ing it. Her parents were nameless and she couldn't recognise
her siblings. She put the glassy, silent spikes of an itchy pod
on the bathroom towels, she wrote bad words in lemon ink on
every tenth page of the Bible. She broke the new 'modernist'
stained glass windows of the passion down at the local. That's
what Father called their Church, their local. It was a gall of a
building with stained glass at one end to make it Church-like.
On that May Day the scales fell away, she chanted.

*

Vaccination Day at school. TB. May Day again. It might be
Perth by this stage. The sign of. Lucida and Duke matched up.
As she's pricked one of the other girls shows Lucida a picture
of her own mother, who is secretary of a gun club. There's the
mother, holding a high-powered rifle, with pictures of Big Game
on the mantelpiece behind her. She looks swishy, like an advert,
her hair and headband perfect and her smile a piece of surrealism. Lucida knows art when she sees it. It's one of her mantras.
She's accumulating as she reads Agatha Christies from the second-hand book exchange down on Railway Avenue (yes, yes, it
must have been Perth), run by the Father Christmas of Old who
is still offering her boiled lollies to go out the back room though
she's fourteen. She stares at him through eyeliner and lipstick and
her cheeks bloom with the lipstick circles she's eyed into place.
Then he says, You'll get thirty cents back on each of those if you
exchange. She never exchanges. She hoards.

The ladder in the art storeroom. A fallen mirror. Mr T. and
his sad, sad personal story. What his wife did to him, leaving
him with the kids and going off just like that, wasn't right. Gotta
cut him some slack. In the storeroom. Climbing the ladder. The
fallen mirror on the floor. His eyes moving from heaven to hell,
hell to heaven. That simple. All his pain accruing. First time?
May Day, of course. Honing objectivity, she looked down at
him looking up into her body and said, This is art, I know it

when I see it.

*

Becoming all too cognisant of her becoming Duke, she measured her existence in steps – goal setting. As she marked her height on the doorframe, she marked her growth of artistic awareness in the place of no reason. Duke would approve she said, tossing the Queen's deadly apple from hand to hand. But I am me, I am so very real. I feel everything I feel walking into a room, eyes swivelling in my direction. I compel, she thought. Interviewing a band in the green room of the Entertainment Centre for her university guild magazine, she said to the lead guitarist who had a bold green mohawk, Your hair reminds me of the Hawk Block being chopped down as we speak. What the fook is the Hork Blok? It's art, darling, art, she said, and made her choice. She was always making her choice/s.

She is twenty-one. Her first visit to Ohio and the Columbus Art Gallery is staging a small show of an Australian artist who is pushing the envelope. Of what? She's curious. DUKE is blazoned. He was in Cow Town for the exhibition opening but is long gone now. Back to the *boo-oosh,* the woman at the desk tells Lucida. She laughs a long slow laugh when she says 'bush.' How on earth did he end up getting an exhibition here? asked Lucida, who could tell the woman was offended on many levels and in many ways but wasn't completely sure what they were. That's Lucida's take, anyway. He was a visiting artist at the university, she said. He followed the Ohio State football team. A Buckeye through and through. Thru and thru!

Lucida studied Duke's paintings and sculptures very closely. The exhibition was entitled 'No World Held Within Here.' Snow. Maple trees. Steep hills. Figures moving through the stillness. She knew she would be furious with Duke's father for paying him so much attention, tooling him up, training him in the pieties and skills of *technique.* She knew this as closing time tossed her out on her ear.

*

Duke, why don't you embrace the nothingness?

What kind of question is that, Lucida? I haven't got time for this.

Duke, why don't you eat the apples I brought all the way out here for you while they're still edible.

Not hungry.

You don't eat, Duke. You're a wraith.

Lucida, can't you concentrate for a minute? Now, watch what I do with this charcoal. So much is in the making of shadows. This is charcoal from my own campfire.

I have a pocket mirror in my handbag – inside my compact. Paint me a self-portrait, Duke, so I have something to remember you by.

Give the barometer over there by the bed a tap, Lucida, will you . . . Needle seems to be stuck.

*

The Ex said, Coffee table books are aesthetically worthless anyway. Show-pony stuff. It's an insult to Duke's memory. He'll be rolling in his grave, You're a talentless freeloader making your home anywhere there's attention to latch onto, Lucida, love. All these idiots lapping up your every word and publishing your every thought, just want a bit of what they imagine you've got. And whatever you think you've got, it's stolen anyway. I *know*, Lucida.

Lucida wasn't going to show that the barb had found its mark. She said, blandly, Home is where the coffee table book is. She wanted to hit the Ex over the head with one of the weighty tomes, but she restrained herself. The snotting would come later.

The beauty of temporal awareness – biding time is an exercise in certainty. Logical. It delighted her Duke would be all diurnal in his coffin with eyes no longer there to roll. She signed another forehead. She poisoned another eye. She managed to touch-up the violinist as the muso threaded her way carefully out of the spiral where she'd blown the audience away with her fantasias on Lucida's variations on Duke's last will and testament. The halogen lights burned hot and somewhere coal was being chewed up and converted to dark air for her and her acolytes to breathe in deeply, to breathe in with excitement and guilt-free pleasure. Oyster. World.

Lucida's DNA

IT STRUCK LUCIDA that she could overcome the impression that she owed all to Duke by subsuming Duke's DNA into her own. She approached a geneticist of great repute and asked her to conduct a modification – to make of Lucida a glowing jellyfish, to give her a taste of Dolly but with long life. In fact, Lucida was planning ahead to Eternity, and this was a first step. She had no desire to look like the Mona Lisa, but Orlan was always on her mind. She had a vial of Duke's blood taken pre-death and a vial taken post-death, though this was, of course, dust, as Duke's remains remained 'unlocated.' She imagined these blood samples might give different effects, but was aware she was coming to this through abstraction – pure art! – rather than through science. Still, Orlan relied on medical hypocrisy to make herself a vision of what people might want to see, so why not? Lucida didn't need surgery to get the chin of Botticelli's Venus, she already had one. Everyone in the art world said so, especially her 'Boys.' They insisted. She once visited Orlan's 'reliquary of flesh' and laughed louder than Orlan. What would Orlan do with Duke's failed penis? What did *Duke* do with it?

What Actually Goes Through Lucida's Mind: a snapshot

I HAVE WATCHED too many performances. I am performance. But I am shy. That is an endearing quality. It is right to feel humility. How can I make it *all* add up. *Das Boot* needed a lead female under pressure. The tricks of representation. I will give this beggar a dollar and hope I am noticed by those that count. What's the point of largesse if it's not a performance? The beggar notices, but he can never be satisfied. Kate Bush doesn't really remember Π outside the studio and if she does it's a mnemonic disconnected from its actuality. Sure of that. Kim Gordon singing about the quarter the woman gives 'her' to put in the washing machine. I was filthy in the gutter – motivation to stay sober. Though a couple of lines wouldn't go astray. The flippancy shows that I am well past my addiction. I could manage. I feel warm and twitchy and buzzy and *creative!* Grab an espresso and don't hang around to be gawked at. They all know who I am. I am watched. I *am* facial recognition. Shit, my feet are aching. Might walk in my stockings, got a spare set in my bumbag. Squeeze a lot into that designer tardis. I could go my own label. Lucida Intervalla. Style. Guru. Something's missing. It's all so fucking boring. That's not original which is what makes it a beautiful label. Think I need to let Roger go. Gorgeous euphemism: Roger, I've got to let you go. Sorry to disappoint, darl, but it's time for you to move on. You've got a lot to do elsewhere. It's a trap, this body thing. How to do body and move away from body at once. Hormones are old old old. I am thinking, maybe, of something out of Chaucer. The Parliament of Birds. I mean, how much love have I really known. Duke invested too much in the possibility of me. My coming. Such a male joke. Like tits instead of boobs. Attention seeker. Duke! I wonder if he can hear me. No, of course he can't. And if he can he's telling no one. No intrepid detective on my heels. Bare feet. Stockings. I've heard of worms entering through the feet. Disgusting. Such a small earth. What did Duke expect: something so small is inevitably going to get damaged, it doesn't take much. Eyes down, s/he's noticing. Value adding. I'll spurn. Those little angels, cats, after birds on those branches. Trees in the middle of the mall. Now, that's affected. Foundation tree. That beautiful piece of propaganda. Picnic baskets. Mrs Dance. Soldiers. I think I will do a book of fantasias on that painting. I love propaganda. I am the tired hunter of collectibles. My apartment in this town is too small. I don't really like watching television. I think my stockings have worn through already. Shoes back on, ughhh, fucking uncomfortable. Have to wear heels though. I am not writing a poem. Okay, in here for an espresso. Have it standing, quick. They're all fixated on me. Smile. What I'd like to do to them all. Surgery on a mass scale. Hmmm. I am sick of being alone. But people are so fucking stupid, so fucking boring. Duke was just like that Chinese poet who was *banal* and wrote about lice and butchering raptors. All weird and out of synch and low-life fascinated. What was I thinking? Where did that go? Early onset. Gives me a shudder. Smile, place cup on counter. Leave. Perfect balance. All legs and short skirt. He looked so crushed, Duke, as if it had all ended anyway. His awareness of my presence. A crash. But I wasn't going to let it turn into a market crash, was I. I am the best conversation I know. Duke on his bed staring at the rippling, boiling ceiling. Becoming whatever it was in his fucking Jindyworobak mind. Orlan feeds her lust with her own flesh and calls it whatever. I know. I know. She's not fooling me but I'll smile anyway. That's ideology and reality. Her truths serve her and her followers fine. What they need to be. And I need, too. So, crow, Beauty, caw at me in the middle of the street and I'll caw right back at you, Caw CAW CAW. What the fuck are you lot looking at! No, suppress, play it straight. Keep cawing and then walk off, smiling, strut your stuff. Assholes. Builder's bum. I'd fuck you bastards then preserve your pricks in aspic. Poor old Duke, what could he do? He wanted nothing so badly. Send a tweet: Absolute good of myself! Let it run. Ninety thousand followers. Must get the boys to grow that a little. Fuck, look at these. Boys aren't on the job. Missed calls – twenty. Phone off. I don't need to be an appendage. Not now. Duke had never touched a mobile phone. They are an offence before God, he'd said. A beautiful ontology. An exquisite atheism. Must tweet that, too, and copyright. Taylor, gal, your greed is an inspiration, your vanity a joy, and your machine about as good as it gets. Never heard you sing, but why the hell would I want to? Your art is your being. O the time of God and his paradoxes and where do I fit into the knowledge? This power I wield in my heels, on the coffee table, in my very DNA, soon to be infused with Duke. Think I will use these tickets to the Goldberg Variations tonight. Love that piece. Could play it once. Should never have given up. Could have been a virtuoso, Mother, I could . . . if I'd practiced rather than fucking and drugging and chasing rock groups around. I like the artiste . . . she's gorgeous. Who to take at such short notice. Yes, our violinist! I will get one of the boys to arrange it. Fuck these shoes are uncomfortable. I'll have blisters for tonight. That espresso has put some zip in my stride. Wouldn't mind a line or two. Shouldn't. Not really. Counterproductive. Twelve steps. Duke, Duke, are you my higher power. Shit. People are looking at me laughing. Okay to be seen smiling, but never laughing. Not real laughter. But it's funny. It's all so fucking funny. I'll tweet 'Love thy neighbour.' Let's see what that does to the followers.

Risk to the Status Quo: Unbelievably a Newer Ben has Become a Detective Operating on a Hunch

SHE HASN'T RECOGNISED me, standing beside her, waiting to order a coffee. And yet, she knew all there was to know about me. Then. Now she knows nothing. She can't see the past, only imagine a future.

I speak loudly to the barista. I am one ahead of her in the queue. I say, The lady can go first. Once she would have called me a sexist pig, but now she just smiles with her Botticelli chin and steps right up and demands her espresso. She is famous for being famous. She is famous because of her pursuit and bottling of Duke. I know she did him. Knocked him off his perch. No evidence, but she doesn't mind the suggestion. Done her no harm. But I know. I have one of the extra passport photos taken in the booth at the beginning of her stepping out. She has – had? – one of mine. We shared needles. We slept together with a rock star in the Sheraton. We told stories of childhood perversities. We aspired. We read *Double Indemnity* aloud and shared a beanbag.

Call it premonition. I never frequent this place. Halfway upmarket. Starched cloths and shirts and short dresses even in the morning. Sugar cubes in wrappers because they transcend. Phones ablaze. Eyes to the screen. Chatter out of the side of mouth. Switchback eyes. And her, standing on heels, seamed red stockings, a zigzag of pink through her hair. Watching us all watching. She is not suspicious, so why not stare. I stare. I don't know her now, but *know* her. I get caught in this. I know she said

133

she'd give that dealer who ripped us off a hotshot if she could get in close enough. And he died. I know she threatened to dob in another when she wouldn't give her credit, and he was raided a few days later. And both of us passed through it all without an arrest, without a record. I'll watch over you, Ben, darling, she said. And she did. I should thank her – I am where I am because of her foresight.

She's quick. Down the hatch. I could follow her but I won't. I've some shopping to do. Need a new tie for the concert tonight. Going with my wife and our oldest son who's a piano prodigy. And he dotes on the harpsichord and Bach. There's no refusing him or my wife. He likes to wear suits – fine suits – and they don't come cheap.

Duke's Dance During Death

POOR LUCIDA. WHITHER shall she wander. Narratives suck in death like there's no tomorrow. I ring a ring a rosie here, till the cows come home. Will-o-the-wisp, ball lightning, a vacuum. Socrates's wisdom a doormat. Overhearing what you don't want to overhear. The knowledge of how and why brings me no solace. In fact, it fits the logic of life perfectly. This voicelessness. Absurdity. These tracks I trudge in circles, my face mouthless, eyeless. The explorer (nearby) tells me there's no time like tomorrow. He's dusty with discovery. He laments every discovery he has made. One fewer for me to make in the future. You see, he says, Australia has a vicarious death sentence. Executions carried out overseas. Executions on home turf called 'deaths.' It's conquest, this art business, he says. I was an official war photographer. I sketched in the battle zones. I marched with the ANZACS. My sister married an American serviceman when he returned to Perth to collect her. They married in America but there was an engagement party on the foreshore at Crawley Bay, outside the university. Pelicans flew six overhead, a flotilla. We all pointed and said Catalan Flying Boats! The war lingered. I caught up with her in the States but none of the rest of the family ever saw her. I have been searching for the desert mole and the night parrot, but I am no biologist. I am an explorer. I have supped on Agent Orange. I let him tell the tales. I can only listen, really. Lucida is speaking for me, busy as always. Our brief acquaintance seems to have occupied so much of her living self. She has some time left to run with it. Leave her be. Let her have her moments. She is an explorer, too, and death invades all narratives. Forgiveness is hardly relevant. She maintains Copenhagen was never part of my life outside the odd exhibition opening.

Lucida: A Mental Snapshot at 2 a.m.

WHERE THE FUCK is she? She should be in the office now. She's bloody American – Americans are always in their offices making time count, making money! What time is it in New York? 1 p.m. Another long liquid lunch. Gotta get some cash flow happening. Disappointing, the violinist. What more is there to say. I hate this tired awake. And what a little prig in his Little Lord Fauntleroy suit. And that hideous mother of his poking her way in front to introduce him to the musician. Right in front of me. Un-fucking-forgivable. And his creepy father lurking in the background watching me out the corner of his eye in a distinctly different way. Unadmiring would be to put it kindly. What did he look like? Fuck, what's happening to my brain cells? Nondescript. That's what he looked like. Might whiz up some carrot juice in the blender. Feed the brain.

Some of Lucida's Best Friends

ACCUSED OF RACISM, Lucida did the exhibition entitled *Some of My Best Friends*. Each *friend* was photographed and their portrait placed in a pink frame. This performative exhibition made her extra famous. She was a force to be reckoned with, and no critic could outflank her – waiting in the wings were her legion of fans and supporters. When vilified by the Christian Right, she converted a prominent gallery into a church, dressed in religious garb, and offered communion to her fans. Grape juice became the vogue and the world was slightly more sober for an instant. Pictured in first class of a Dreamliner dressed and painted green, she became the poster person for The New Green Movement. She flew from capital to capital speaking on behalf of a green planet. Green paint became all the rage. It was that simple, and she knew it. I am the lifeblood of the educated, she wrote in blood over a famous painting in the Louvre, adding so much more value to it, and receiving the Légion d'honneur almost instantly. She became the face of Non-Muslim France, and the face of Muslim France. She wore a burkini after it had been banned, and was praised. She went naked along the main drag in Tehran. She survived it all and blossomed. She told the world she no longer suffered from anxiety and would cure the biosphere's sickness without costing governments a cent. She drank with Houellebecq in a cafe opposite Notre Dame and was photographed spitting in his drink while he went for a piss against the wall. He should always be watching over his shoulder, she said. That's what his works tell us. And I am the cult to end all cults. Why is he getting into the public or pubic bed with me? Sales? Nothing so easy. Credibility. But I have plenty, he's welcome to some of it. I just exacted the price. The piss, the spit, the ha ha ha.

*

Some people read too much into history, she said, rebuffing the persistent man who claimed that history showed she was wrong in most things.

And what kind of name is Lucida? Sounds like Lucifer. *He* was a bore. And Lucida had no time for bores. She could easily ask The Boys to encase the Devil in concrete and call the exhibit *Houdini: Get Out of this One.* It had a ring to it.

Look, she said, I don't know you outside your predilection for anal sex, but you know me. That puts me at a disadvantage. Your anonymity appealed to me but doesn't any longer. I like your open sports shirt and the fact you twilight sail on the river with your mates, but who *are you* precisely?

I am an engineer. I have just won pre-selection for a safe seat. I am anti-refugee, pro-business, pro-mining, anti-funding for climate change science, and pro the use of coal. I wish to abolish unions and am a born again Christian. I was in the SAS. That's it, my resume!

And you pick women up as they walk along the river watching the South Perth ferry ply to & fro, to & fro?

Yes, it's a hobby. Gee, you've got *long* legs. They're all out of proportion with the rest of your body? How tall are you anyway?

You are a rude man, aren't you. And you've got *short* stubby and very hairy legs.

Women tell me they're masculine legs.

Well, you *are* a man, aren't you?

You've got a nice arse though.

You're a charmer, through and through.

You're a bit old for me.

Christ, you must be twenty years older than me.

Still, it's man's choice, isn't it.

Aren't you afraid I'll go to the media. Or just send a tweet?

Tell them your dirty doings. You're a married man.

Sure. But you won't. And if you're as famous as you say it won't do you any good either.

It's astonishing you don't know. Where have you been? Under the rocks you mine? No, I won't tell, though if I did it would only enhance my reputation. Now . . . what's this here? Do you like the work of Margaret Preston?

Who?

She was an artist. A great artist. You have a reproduction of some of her work on your signet ring. A sweet little flower with bite. How on earth did you come across a ring like that? Not really very he-man!

Oh, some grateful constituents gave it me when I opened a new art gallery a few months ago. Looks nice, doesn't it. The woman who does them – a real looker, actually – does copies of paintings in the W.A. Art Gallery. They're nasturtiums, I think. Not very accurate, but I guess that's art. Modern art that is. Inaccurate. I don't like all this talk. Back on your hands and knees, puppy, and let's try again.

I'm sore, mister. You've ridden this filly enough for one day.

Shut up bitch, he said, playfully but meaning business, and take what you're given! That's it. I'm hard again. Slip on a condom and here we go! Those bloody long legs of yours make the angle all wrong. Drop down a bit, will ya. There!

You're a revelation, said Lucida. Aghhh, Eternuer! Sorry, I have sneezed you out of me! That's a relief. We learn when we least expect to learn. Please don't throw the used condom on the floor. It's filthy. Yes, eternity. ETERNITY! You're a revelation, darl. You make me feel humble. I'd forgotten the feeling. You're a real pig, and I'm an expert on these things. Someone will take you down down down one of these days, buster.

Ha! the women rarely complain. Rarely complain. I'll tell you what, babe, you can come twilight sailing with me sometime.

Raincheck that, darl. I've got work to do.

And the very next day, Lucida has The Boys track some of The Beast's earlier conquests who were more than willing to spill the beans on a number of pertinent websites. And Lucida also had The Boys whip up a new Margaret Preston signet ring wallpaper. The originating designer got a small percentage, as did the Preston estate.

*

It was disappointing when outrage turned too quickly and too unprofitably to acceptance. When she first hinted that Duke, maybe, just maybe, wasn't actually Danish, but came from the small southwest coastal town of Denmark the world's art press and The Guardian newspaper expressed outrage. The Danish ambassador was recalled from Australia and the foreign minister contacted Lucida's office with a *please explain*, but with the please explain expressed very very gently. So Lucida provided a grainy Polaroid of a small boy on a pedalo in the Denmark River, a big smile on his face, sitting next to a woman who could have been his mother or an auntie or an older sister or a family friend. Without explanation, she said, Here is the evidence. And though Denmark, the nation state, would continue to claim Duke as their own, and though art critics always considered his work in terms of his Danish influences (especially Vilhelm Hammershøi and Asger Jorn), and his influence on contemporary Danish artists, especially Tal R, was never questioned, they all *subliminally* wrote of him as being a sou'-west coast and forest boy from the tall timbers and hippy commune milieu. Lucida enriched the discourse by coming up with some pastel drawings on suitably aged paper showing karri trees and massive tinglewoods reaching towards the sky – nothing technical about them, just good honest plein air moments, a truth in itself. And at the tops and bottoms of the pages were sweet little marsupial motifs that looked like they'd been copied off souvenirs. They were calm, peaceful pictures that spoke of harmony and exquisite banality in the world. Vegans and pacifists claimed him for their own, which repulsed Lucida, but she let it ride. It came so easy. All of it.

Lucida's Saga

WHOSE TALE IS this to tell? It's mine now, said Lucida, having instructed The Boys to crib it from any source they might readily access without straining the timetable and resource pool. Nobody here is going to complain. I have some Anglo-Saxon heritage and Svein Forkbeard took most of that territory before he carked it in 1014, and Duke's lies need to be thrown into relief. And so, of the rumblings with King Æthelred, Well King Æthelred took the rack-off-Normie philosophy by the short and curlies, and elsewhere dreamt Forkbeard's toes curling in bed, King Edmund the Holy deploying his wiles, but post-, King Æthelred snapped to it and was back on deck with Olaf the Saint pushing his mate's shit up the hill, relegating the Danes to a thimbleful of what they'd had. But Forkbeard's son Knut progressing from the ripe old age of ten gathering unto him over time the Danes who would pilfer and loot, rape and desecrate, in the ship-wrecker's ways of having his cake, singing Heave, ho, Westwards, sons of Denmark and my royal pals, and then plenty of pilfering and looting and raping and desecrating . . . and burning . . . and King Knute and his allies had their Viking ways with all and sundry and eventually King Æthelred carked it after decades pushing people around and King Knute snaffled Emma, the deceased King's wife whilst she sailed the restless seas, and took her into his bed and sacked her. And on and on it goes, all the way to Centralia. And now a delegation has arrived to suss out the detention centre on Nauru and learn the ways the modern-day tyrants deal with their enemies, to rent-a-spear and shield and breastplate, to act as deterrent to enemies like the nuclear umbrella, in this age of the Viking back with a vengeance quasi-historical fantastical fetishism. One of The Boys footnoted here, in Lucida's charming voice, And those who assist the crossing of our lands by those escaping trauma and destruction will be jailed for treason, and put to the pit. And placing her seal on this saga, Lucida sent it off to her admirers in Canberra who displayed replicas on their office walls and their staff were inspired and enforced the will of the people as embodied in their representative and spokesperson, Lucida. And thus light washed yet again over the land.

Lucida Blackletter

ALL ANGLES AND turns, busted and broken. No antiqua in her cupboard. All new old. This style. She googles and all she searches relating to herself is at the top or high up in the results. She is the algorithm. A sweet little loveheart tattoo with the flying banner below reading *O Fraktur*. Her left buttock. She had it photographed during a happening. Reviving the old forms, playing a UFO Club recording of 'Interstellar Overdrive' during the revelation. Sometimes, she told the crowd, as the event was winding down and their was a static of silence to fill, I like to think of myself as Emily from Syd's song, 'See Emily Play.' I am rich enough now to say it, but it wasn't always that way. I had no silver spoon in my mouth once I deserted the family home/s, which might disqualify me from being Emily in one way as she surely retained her silver spoon, but surely we can all become Emily if we put our minds to it. And then she jiggled her arse, And said to much affectionate laughter, And I will always play! Broken citizen that I am. And she added, with truthful viciousness, You make me famous because you require me, you need to offload your fears and hatreds on the Successful Female. I perform for your delectation. And Lucida, in a quiet moment, a little teary in the bathroom, said to herself, I do this because I have no choice. My outline is getting hazy. Otherwise I will be left playing a role, I will be left at the beck and call of others. I will fail in the machine's beauty contest so I have to make my own way, cut a new path through the shit. I only ever wanted to be a person and this failed. I cannot be a person in the ordinary world. Only fame makes me a person, and more than a person.

Once, when I was visiting a church in provincial France, I encountered a pair of font frogs, Lucida said (back in front of an adoring audience), who looked so exquisite in their garb, that I just had to interview them. They refused and I broke down and cried. They huddled and whispered and genuflected to the cross then stated a fee and out in the brazen sunlight of the wine town I elicited such juicy details of their pasts that I shouted them a meal and drinks at the tourist-friendly cafe in the town square which they had never before frequented. The cafe owner, who clearly despised the font frogs but was deeply curious, flirted with the old girls as well as me. Foolish, foolish man.

So much easier than Carolingian, thought Lucida, showing her tattoo to a group of artists in Frankfurt. They revelled in her cursive, they celebrated her flesh. One anarchist in the group seemed less pleased, less easy to please. He said, A lot of air miles goes into this performance – flashing your ass in country after country. Yes, but Lucida said, My ass has been finding its way home. They all laughed. Even the anarchist. Though his laugh was different. Annoyingly like Duke's but fresher and with a German accent. Lucida was sort-of attracted to him – she knew he was a lie, just like Duke. She smiled her deadly, luscious, killer smile.

In Copenhagen she was given a personal invitation to appear before the Royal Family – the *younger* members. There was an Australian connection there her agent was able to tap into. It didn't take much cajoling to get the 'personal.' She told them, peeling down her jeans to reveal the tattoo in as discreet a manner as protocol dictated, that Duke himself had been her inspiration and that Duke had told her of seeing fire-eaters in the city opposite the fair grounds swallowing fire that never emerged. Some had been children with bellies full of cinders. One of the retainers said, They mustn't have been true Danes. Not Danes of the blood. Lucida stored that gem away for later use. Is it true that Duke was a barbarian? a well-dressed older woman (older but still younger in the context) asked in well-pruned English. Barbaric, maybe, said Lucida, but regretfully, no true barbarian.

*

Hybrids. Lucida had her webmaster place a request on her website for 'old-fashioned letters.' She was sick of electronic mail. The Boys answered that stuff, and would no doubt have to answer conventional mail – where relevant/pertinent/useful/utilitarian – but she wanted to know that people were willing to write to her on paper. Letterheads welcome. She had one of her own made up, handwrote a note of invitation to one and all, had it scanned and placed on the front page of her website. Letters poured in and Australia Post was grateful. They even contacted her agent and said that Lucida had single-handedly given the post people hope. The old ways hadn't died out completely. Some letters were worrying and after showing her, The Boys handed over to the police for further exploitation, but one seemed to display such personal knowledge of her life, such intimate knowledge of her past, and was in a 'hand' she recognised but couldn't quite place, couldn't quite recall from those many years ago when handwriting was not only the vogue but a utilitarian necessity, that she carried it around in her bumbag for days, rereading on street corners, in cafes, and propped up on four pillows with red satin pillowslips on her large round waterbed. It had no 'Dear' and no signing off 'sincerely' or 'love' or 'yours' – it was just a single sheet of minuscule blackletter printing on one thin airletter page (they still exist, she was amazed and pleased to find) postmarked Mount Lawley, Perth. It read:

And so, Lucida . . . if I may . . . I am on your case. But I'll say no more of that. At this stage. I saw your left buttock. The tattoo. It was 1992. You were, what, eighteen then? Publishing your first interviews in fan magazines, following the bands, drooling venom across their egos. What was it you said about politics? About 'ethnicity.' About white punks. About black reggae stars? None of that turned up in your printed pieces, but I heard you say it and I know what's been driving you. The agenda. Protestant work ethic? Sharing needles. The intimacy of blood, eh? You decorated the windows with spew. You sang along with a hotel bed rendition of that hymn. And the intimations of Bluetooth. A lust for Church to weld with State, always. How did that hymn go, girl? That early betrayal of all DUKE stood for. Make you shudder? Premonition? Anti-Climacus. This sin forgiven. You are not the holy spirit, Lucida, you deceiver of fonts. Gathering your tour groups away from the individual. I am me, sister. I am me. I sing this hymn at the Service in Our Saviour. Hear it? Do your research - it was one of his faves. Cite that. Your tyranny of art, your tyranny of self made all of us. You consumed me once and I carry its marks, but I am whole now. I didn't give you genital warts. Your case. Your seatrunk with the labels of all those visited ports. Who am I to judge in my slut self? I know how peer groups work. I know you've needed to make us all your peers. We, looking up even when looking down upon the tattoo on your still beautifully rounded, lily-white bum cheek.

She loved and hated this letter. Who was it speaking to her? Loving and hating *her*? She clutched it to her chest and cried for the joy of mail, for old-fashioned letter writing. She wanted to write back. How? She would write an open letter to the Mount Lawley post office. She would revivify the deadletter office!

Dear Anonymous,

I love you. I have always loved you. Watch out, I might kill you. This is not a threat. This is metaphor. Write me again.

Love,
Lucida (Intervalla) Blackletter

*

She never heard back. But she knew the blackletter writer was close by, close at hand, closing in. I must draw him out in the open, she thought. I must go some place he will have no refuge.

I will head outback. I will go to the edge of a red desert and he will find me. Or she. Or they. Though the letter was all he-speak. But it could be neither he nor she. I am open to the possibility. I will establish grounds for creativity. For it to all fall in place. On the edge of the red desert. With tektites and desert animals that find water in very rare and specialised ways. I will trace spirals in the redness. I will take my camera. I will travel to honour Duke. I will go alone. I will take my satellite phone. I will drive a new Jeep. I will obtain endorsements. It all so beautifully adds up.

An Artist's Impression of Duke and Lucida Together at Sunset

Lucida came across this in a regional gallery in Victoria and rang her solicitor (not her QC – she had a full legal team by now) immediately. He recommended she and her agent come to a deal with the amateur painter to have it reproduced in her workshop, to take it to a whole new level. The painter wouldn't resist. The art is in the copying, Lucida said, and her solicitor said, I understand. And the subject takes control of her destiny inside art which is inside everything, she added. This is the future world in which I am involved and there is no future which is not me, she said loud so all in the gallery looked around. She smiled her silver smile and said to them all, This goldmining town of yesteryear is living in a time warp, I will bring it life.

*

The portrait was a landscape. There was Lucida in skinny jeans, legs climbing above the occasional stunted Myall tree, and there was the lake glistening pink and white crystal with the sun's rays shooting hope over the aridity. Small birds were at her feet, which were bound in hiking boots. And there was Duke, naked, wearing thongs on his feet, which were large, gripping the sanding lake-edge with authority. His body wavered around the genitals and his chest caved in and then his shoulders were suddenly and surprisingly broad if you climbed his body from feet up which you did, but his head was small to Lucida's large memento mori skull. It has such a haunting effect, said Lucida to The Boys. We'll stylise that a little. It's not a beauty contest. People will think I've embraced integrity. People will see my depth. This projected past will be all our nows and our futures. I am *of*. They are of me. Duke equivocates in memory. Who is he? We know Lucida. She stretches way above us all. She is beyond gender, ethnicity and history itself. She is science. She is culture.

Lucida instructed The Boys to place name tags in a Gothicky script next to her and Duke. Duke's name was illegible.

*

Lucida would never admit to being jealous of Hanna B., but she noted how much attention the author was getting from the Murdoch media. I would never want to meet her, Lucida told herself, It would sully me. But thinking over her issues with Hanna B. over and over, Lucida decided attack was the best approach. She would write her *own* work of fiction. I will not destroy her world, I will take it lock stock and barrel. I will conserve and protect what I have taken.

Lucida sat down with The Boys and they sketched out a simple tale of two children lost in the desert who meet a Guide and she shows them to the Special Place where there is water and food and they are rewarded for their virtue. It's all in the names we give the characters, she told The Boys. Let's go for Miss Flossy and Master Mungbean and Mother Star. And, being on a roll, she said, and let the tale begin Under the Big Blue Daytime Sky and under the Big Star-lit Night, they remembered they'd played together in a sandpit with cars buzzing close by, kicking up a din, but note, there was a silence they were afraid of . . . Over to you, now boys. But don't gild the lily – keep it short and sweet and simple. Know thy formula.

Hachette, who worshipped Lucida, published it in a first print run of three million copies which took out a large chunk of forest. They had plenty more earmarked. They stuck the 'mixed sources' label in the front of the book, and assured the world they were all 'well-controlled'. The e-version ate the energy from a dozen power stations around the world. The world grew old in the light of this simple, archetypal tale. Simple as that. Lucida's agent said, as they signed a deal for an illustrated version, You have mastered whimsy and quirkiness, Lucida! Lucida actually blushed and her tongue poked slightly and endearingly out through her lush, strangely inflated lips.

*

Worn out with her labours, Lucida decided to Go On Retreat. She wished to move above the Ninefold Heaven but to also have a moment to herself. She flew back to Perth and went into The Hills. Meditating, she watched her fellow participants out the corner of her eye. Consulting the Great Work that was imprinted on her brain from her younger days, she sought out and embraced the slimy in all things. The slimy is at work in all of them, in all these retreaters. I imagine the icicle. I feel the icicle. I know the icicle. It is a material being. I embrace my materiality. I consume me. And Lucida rose up, and strode on her long legs over the floor, over the mats, bumping the odd meditator, and on out of the building to her Prius parked under a marri tree dropping honkynuts like epiphanies onto the roof of the car with soft, plosive thuds. Carnaby's Cockatoos – a species almost extinct – making a ruckus in the canopy, preparing to fly because the weather was changing.

*

Asked to address Parliament, Lucida chose to speak on 'Looking Up Close.' She told the representatives of the people that they must examine a blade of grass, consider an ant, and read her soon-to-be released memoir, which she was sure they could all manage because it was only ten thousand words long, in big print, and available on all e-reader formats, illustrated, and written with a vocab that a nine-year-old could certainly comprehend. She got a good laugh out of this. But then she said, No, *really* . . . and they all felt grave and introspective on their shiny leather seats.

*

New Ben was sitting in the public gallery when Lucida made her address to Parliament. It took a lot of string-pulling to get there. But he was quite senior now in the Federal Police and strings are there to be pulled. And he pulled them. Hard. He squirmed a little as he listened to her confident wisdoms, and he almost admitted to himself that he still felt that unhealthy, disturbed and slightly dirty attraction that had made him her lapdog when they were O so very young, but it also hardened him with resolve. The bodies she has left behind her! he thought. The trail of destruction she doesn't even feel. As if under a permanent dose of novocaine – no matter how close to the root of herself she drills she doesn't feel it. She will leave no record. Not even her private thoughts will be breached. She lives in a perfect hebephrenia. He shuddered again and felt firmish and sticky down *thar*, down below.

A Glimpse of Ben's Childhood

HE DIDN'T WANT to play football, but his father insisted. That is, his father wanted him to play football because his father no longer could. Baz Murphy had been a star full forward, a major goal kicker for the town's football team, the Cougars. And here was his son, Ben, going on and on about the name of the club, which was a piss off. A cougar is a fast and dangerous animal, Ben. But Dad, I mean seriously, there's no cougars living here . . . not anywhere in the whole of Australia. People don't think about things like that, snapped his father. Baz had little tolerance for abstract discussion. His son was going to play for the Junior Cougars, and that was all there was to it!

They lived just outside town. A farm edging the town was a difficult thing. People resented the spray, the harvest . . . they encroached, as Baz said. But it also made people envious of all that land, *their* land. Baz wouldn't hear any of this bullshit about land rights and refused to listen to Welcome to Country at official events. But to Ben, it was just *awkward* – he was supposed to ride his bike into town . . . not far enough out for the school bus, not really, though when it was raining he did catch it, sheltering in the old rainwater tank that lay lidless on its side, running out as he heard the bus approach. But it was a Saturday and raining and his father was out ploughing and his mother was down in the city seeing Ben's nanna who was unwell. So he had to ride his bike even though it was drizzling. To the town oval, which was on the far side of town. And arriving there, soaked, the studs of his football boots weirdly slipping off the bike pedals, he saw

a bunch of his friends and enemies huddled under the tin-shed
overhang. Coach was the sports teacher from school, with whom
Ben had a so-so relationship.

Glad you could make it, Ben! said the teacher with his usual
sarcastic meaninglessness. Ben sidled up next to a schoolmate,
bobbling on the slim bit of concrete under the overhang.

Now, boys . . . we're going to practise our skills. Out there!

Ben said to a sort-of friend, I hate this, my Dad makes me
do it. Stupid game. His sort-of-friend said, Same here. Down in
the city they get to play soccer and baseball. That's what I'd like
to be doing. Ben agreed, because it was the easiest thing to do,
but he didn't want to be playing any sport. He had no interests.
But the city *was* appealing. Last time he'd been down there he'd
gone to the movies and seen *Poseidon Adventure* with his nanna.
His nanna had sat on the end of the row and Ben had had to sit
next to a weird girl who had dyed black hair with a silver streak
through it. She kept poking Ben in the ribs during the movie,
and Ben yelled, Get out of it! and his nanna told him to *Shoosh*.
The girl bugged him the whole time then when the film was
finished and they were getting up out of their seats, she emerged
from the darkness into the light and said, Hold on, wait. And
then she took a small notebook from her handbag – she was the
first girl of roughly his own age he'd ever seen with a handbag
or on her own at a cinema – and scribbled down something and
handed it to him. Ring me sometime, she said. What was that all
about Ben? asked his nanna suspiciously. Nothing, Nanna. But
Nanna gave him one of her looks of distaste, as if she'd sucked
on a lemon, so Ben added incredulously, She's from my school,
she gave me a message for a mate of mine. The lemon face got
worse but they were being pushed up the aisle by the crowd and
the likelihoods and facts and deceptions were lost in the press.
They went to a coffee shop afterwards and Ben had Black Forest
Cake. Ben! Concentrate, willya! Pick up the ball, pick up the
ball! Your Dad would have something to say if he could see this.
Come on, get with the programme! And Ben was playing footy
with the rest of the boys and working on his skills and doing
precisely what coach told him to do.

*

Attempting to smoke rolled-up newspaper, Ben set fire to the horse paddock. There were no horses in the horse paddocks – Ben had never seen horses in the horse paddock – but birds flew away fast and insects were consumed. Ben tried to stamp it out and burnt his sandshoes and legs, and then the rapidly expanding fire threatened to eat him alive so he ran and ran as the sickly looking smoke rose higher into the wavering sky. The stubble fire stopped at the firebreaks, but his father called out the bush fire brigade as soon as he smelt smoke and saw the plume, and was down there himself with the water truck faster than lightning which was how the farm nearly burnt to the ground a couple of summers earlier. Baz Murphy eventually tracked down Ben, dragged him to the firebreak of the horse paddock, beat the truth out of him. He beat Ben in front of the bush fire brigade who by and large thought Ben had it coming. Gotta learn, Baz. You're right there. Can't have a budding arsonist on our hands. And then Baz emptied his beer fridge and sat with the boys from the fire brigade, sat on upturned cut-off twenty-two-gallon oil drums, and drank into the evening, keeping an eye on the charred horse paddock in case an unseen ember rose and took out the district.

*

Ben was sent to board at Guildford Grammar under the power pylons when he was fourteen. It was then he rang the number the girl had given him. It was a city number. It was two years later and he doubted she'd be there. Someone picked up the phone and he asked for the name that had been on the notepaper, which, along with the phone number, was burnt into his brain. Is Lucida there? No answer then the sound of the phone being put down then some mumbling then a girl answering, Yeah, this is Lucida, who is this?

Lucida on Her Way to the Outback to Raise the Spirit of Duke Runs into a Popular Novelist in a Small Wheatbelt Town

LUCIDA QUITE LIKED driving. Nothing better than a drive 'nowhere,' out into the country, along long straight roads. She had a lovely Toyota Prius that made her fans smile with approval. She is sensitive to the planet, they'd say. And she felt she was. She could have owned Ferraris – many Ferraris – by this stage. But this was a pilgrimage. She was heading out to the edge of the arid zone to make contact with the spirit of Duke. She would be far away from where Duke passed, but she knew she'd find him anywhere 'out there,' occupying the ETERNAL space with his presence.

The route would take her through some larger wheatbelt towns and some very small ones. Three hours into her drive she pulled into a gothic looking town on the railway, its main street all brown-red corrugated iron peaked roofs and busted walls. There were wheat silos, there was a museum of grain growing, there was a cold beer and skimpy barmaid sign outside the pub which was built in a confusion of colonial styles. A hairdresser. A co-op. A farmer's trading post. A shire office. And, strangely she thought, a small art gallery cum bookshop on a corner edged by smashed up asbestos houses. She just *had* to pull over. Her eye had also been drawn to the spanking new BMW sports parked too close to the corner and a few feet out from the kerb. She felt envious – what's that doing out here? And it's so shiny – no dust at all. Not off a farm. I shouldn't be so rigid . . . the Prius is a dog of a car.

She parked and sauntered in. The late-middle-age woman behind the counter, well groomed, was talking with a forty-something woman dressed in designer leather. Lucida marvelled over the leather woman's hair which looked like it had been covered in varnish. What product is that? she wondered. Lucida was attracted and repelled at once. This is mannequin art, she told herself. The woman turned and faced her eye to eye. It was Hanna B., *the historical novelist*.[6] She was often in the same magazines as Lucida, and sometimes they pushed each other off front covers. But Hanna B. was a Sydney girl who now lived in New York. Lucida was excited and sick. Too many conjunctions were swirling through her brain. And though she'd never met her in person, she said, Hanna!, and Hanna said, Lucida! Howcome? asked Lucida. Research, said Hanna, Adding, a touch of the authentic – one of my characters moves here in 1946 and I am trying to get the inside running. Oh, that's good, said Lucida. And you? Well, said Lucida, I am heading out to the desert to make contact with Duke. But Duke's dead, darling? Yes, said Lucida, He is dead, but his spirit . . . Yes, yes, darling, I understand . . . That Duke, said Hanna, was always *so* spiritual. So close to the earth. Aboriginal, almost, darling. Lucida, not above such exploitation herself, cringed a little in the mirror of *herself* – her outline ached. She felt she should say something to correct the bigotry but honestly didn't know what to say. Yes, she said again . . . yes, yes, yes! All these exclamations. All these affirmations. She was giddy with emphasis. This is a happening, she told herself, but which one of us is going to ask for the selfie first. It mattered. But the tension was broken a little and the problem solved a little when the neat women behind the counter said, Photo op! Of you two, then the three of us, then one of you two outside my shop! It wasn't a question and the relieved celebrities complied without hesitation.

*

6 Reader, it's hard to tell if this is the same Hanna B. that had been obsessing Lucida earlier. As we know, there are many Hanna Bs out there.

The Prius and the BMW were certainly covered in dust by the time they reached the shopkeeper's house. Her name was Beryl. Another era, said Lucida, rubbing it in. Hanna had accepted the invitation for both of them – they were sisters in sophistication, fame and fortune. Authenticity, said Hanna. Lucida, not one to follow a sister, thought she'd get the upper hand at some point and make it all work for her. But in the meantime she put the weirdness of events down to the journey of life.

Over tea and scones, Beryl told the women that her hubbie and eldest son would soon be in from the outer reaches of their enormous farm. My son is in his final year of medicine and is spending his holidays studying and helping his father. We have three employees, but it's always nice when the father and son team reunite. Conjunctions, Lucida told herself.

The husband looked like an aged Ned Kelly. Something about him – something quite Duke, actually. Maybe he was the reason Lucida was there with Hanna and Beryl. Hanna had latched on to the son, who looked like a rugged white male model. He was very very hunky. Hanna had turned him into a character within a few words and was already at his heels as he promised to show her around the machinery sheds and shearing shed. Stinks in there, he said, And your heels will get stuck between the boards. No problem, said Hanna, I carry flats in the car. Can we make a slight detour and I'll change into them. Lucida imagined that short leather skirt discreetly opening as Hanna changed her shoes sitting in the driver's seat, talking to him the whole time about this and that.

Ned was talking to her, Lucida, about art. He seemed uncannily knowledgeable for a farmer. He knew Juniper. He collected Indigenous art. She followed him into the lounge room which turned out to be a spectacular gallery. The missus isn't keen on this stuff, he said, but I like it a lot. Some real talent around here – two of my workers are artists. It's their land, you know. Not that Beryl acknowledges it, but our son does. You know, he might even give it back when we're gone.

Lucida was dumbstruck. Fuck, she thought, what do I do with this? Anomaly. Weirdness. She felt sad. Then she knew she was trapped and there was only one way out. She began a conversation with him about vermin on the property – the very large property of twenty thousand acres as it turned out – and how it was dealt with. Do you poison with 1080? she asked. You're knowledgeable, he laughed. I am, Lucida said, I am. And then there was Beryl hovering at their elbows, suddenly nervous, asking Lucida if she would like to meet Mrs Dora Heising, one of their 'local' artists – her paintings were in the gallery, you might have noticed. And Lucida had, thinking at the time that she could send The Boys up to stage and intervention, blitz the walls and paintings with spray-painted tags, photograph, and she'd take it from there. Her workshop. *Her* studio. Dora was a landscape painter who specialised in local flowers, though Ned was telling her most of the land was cleared of bush and there weren't many spaces for wildflowers to raise their heads anymore. The tourists still come in small numbers, he said, on a prayer and a whim . . . hoping. It's prayer and a wing, corrected Beryl. That's what I said, said Ned. And then Hanna was in the room with the hunk as well, and she said, *Wing and a prayer*, and its origin is a World War II film. And that's what I am taking about. Just came into to say – in my pumps! – not to wait on me, Lucida, darling, as I am going to be some time looking over the sheds and the property with my wonderful escort. Maybe our paths will cross again, somewhere else in the world. She is wonderfully fatuous, thought Lucida, admiring and loathing at once. Conjunctions. And, Ned, how else do you deal with vermin on your spread?

Lucida Further and Farther Out

FURTHER AND FARTHER out. Out from the focal point of population. The oddity and paradox that is Perth stretching a hundred and twenty kilometres along the coastal plain, but being isolated from the rest of the world's urbanities, played in her thoughts, her recollections. Duke would have said this, Lucida half thought, approaching away from logic. Reaching towards the Absolute. Lucida became all numeric looking at the odometer. She'd fuelled in town after the visit to Beryl's and Ned's place. She'd already forgotten about Hanna whose novels she would never read anyway. She was happy to get away from the crowd on one level, but unhappy on all others. It's the means to my end, she thought. Driving wasn't meditative, she decided, it was draining and braindead. She took to counting the corpses of wildlife on the side of the road. And then driving into the dusk, approaching the final town before going 'out,' the town where she'd arranged for a room in the pub with all the possibilities that might bring, she hit a roo.

Swerving then impacting, the sickening thud, the metal-flesh binary, she heard Duke in her ear: This is your truth. It is truth. Flashing imagery. Blood and fur. Shaking, she steps out and sees her broken passenger-side headlight, the crumpled bonnet. And the reddish buff roo hurled onto the road's shoulder, its head at right angles, looking above it. She poked it with her shoe. It was dead. Mangled and broken-necked. Paws so delicate-looking. And the tail, thicker than her upper arm, her bicep. She thought she would cry but she didn't. She went back to her car, looked at the orange, vacant paddocks around her, and thought that it was uncommonly warm for early spring and that these orange paddocks should at least be tinged green or in crop or something. But they were just dead-looking. This is the Omen of Duke, she told herself. He is my truth.

Lucida had come to a stop near the ten ks from town marker. She started the car. It was getting cold outside. She wanted the heater. The day had been pleasant – tepid, warmish. Nice. The sun was going and the orange and indigo nimbus around the odd scraggly, surviving eucalypt scared her. It was getting dark so rapidly. Looking back over her shoulder, she couldn't even discern roughly where the dead roo lay. Her statistic. The engine was running okay, but as she went to pull back onto the road, a grinding noise came from the front left. The wing was digging into the tyre. She stopped, got out and pulled at the wing to release it from the tyre. It came away enough. She drove on and on until she encountered a town. No one had passed her. In fact, since leaving the farm she'd seen three or four other vehicles. Unsettling.

She pulled into the service station which had two pumps and was about to close – an old white-haired man with a hunch was dragging the signs back through the flystrips. She feared that once over the threshold he'd be lost but she noticed the pumps weren't locked and were still on. She pulled up alongside one and stepping out, inspecting the damage again, she went to him, through the flystrips.

Hit a roo, she said. There were wizened pies in the warmer behind the glassed counter. How much are they? she asked. End of the day, he said, You can 'ave for 'alf price. I will then, she responded. A roo, eh? as he ladled the pies into a brown paper bag. And I'll have a Diet Coke, she added. Okay. Could you look at it? The damage? Well, I'm finishin' up for the day. And then he kinked his head sideways and looked at her, away from her, beyond her, beyond his and her bodies, into the congealing dark, insects at the lights, and said, I could, but it'd cost ya overtime. After hours. That's okay, she said. It's a Prius. A what? A Prius . . . it has batteries and petrol. All of 'em 'ave batteries, dearie. She pushed a pie through the mouth of the bag and said, mid-bite, I'm famished, excuse me. Where is the hotel? Well, dearie, there's me, the hotel, the shop, and three houses . . . oh, and a church which no one goes to. Reckon you'll find it okay. Hmmm, yes, right . . . I'll just grab my bag from the car and leave it with you. She strode out through the flystrips, munching, and the hunched old man followed on, muttering to himself, sniffing at her tail. She continued to a back door and he stood in front of the car, shaking his head and saying, Fuckin' roos, yep, yep, same ol' same ol' . . . Gunna cost ya, dearie, and I can't do no body work. But I might be able to pull it out a bit better and into shape . . . you'll be able to drive it fine but it won't look so pretty. Tyre isn't badly damaged, though I'd suggest you use it for the spare and switch 'em over. I can do that. Will cost you three hundred for my efforts . . . a Prius, eh? One of these eco-logical cars, eh? Only ecology we've got around 'ere are roos. Fuck 'em.

*

The hotel lounge where Lucida sat to a meal, the pies barely having brushed the sides, was almost empty other than two blokes in blue singlets eating massive steaks with no vegetables. They ignored Lucida. She ate her meal self-consciously, speaking loudly and with a slightly different voice from her usual, to the barmaid who was serving between pouring drinks for a few more blokes in the front bar playing pool. The click click click of balls annoyed her. She asked if they had any fruit salad as it wasn't on the menu. Only what's on the menu, luv, said the barmaid who was belle laide and had a strand of copper hair stuck in the corner of her mouth. You're pre-Raphaelite, said Lucida. Whatever you say, luv. One of the blokes finished his steak, smacked his lips loudly, skulled a beer, and pushed his seat back, stretched his legs, and said, That hit the spot. The other bloke kept hacking away at the steak, paying his mate no notice. Bored, the bloke who'd finished finally paid Lucida some attention and said, What

brings you out here, Ms? He said *Ms*. Lucida feigned diffidence
then said, Work. Long way from the city, Ms. Yes, good to get
away, she said. Well, when ya finished maybe you'd like to come
over to the quarters and have a smoke with us? The bloke still
eating choked on his meat.

*

Getting stoned with shearers was a first for Lucida. She'd been
stoned half her life, but not with shearers. She'd been stoned in
the bush, in the desert, in cities. She'd been stoned when Duke
had passed. But never with shearers. She progressed to a completely different level of being. She was anxious, but she didn't
feel sinful. She felt this was a necessary stage in her evolution as
Absolute Artist. Her freedom was tied to her sinning, and she felt
she was justified in anything. What are your names? Adam and
Curly. Curly was bald. Adam had the most pronounced Adam's
apple she'd ever seen. This is good shit, they said. Skunk, said the
other. Looking forward to it, she said, as she pulled a cone fast
and hungrily. They were impressed. This'll rot your socks – you're
gunna fall down down down. They could have both fucked her
that night but weren't interested. They were interested in getting
off their faces. And telling stories. She was willing to listen, and
thus she gained acceptance and was revered and protected.

Curly's Story

Curly's story could have been one of despair but wasn't really. He was resilient, and whatever the 'white bastards' threw at him, he was having none of them. He had a purpose, he said, and was sticking to it.

There's something of the Ben about you, said Lucida.

The what?

Oh, nothing. Continue, she said with a curlicue of her hand.

You're pretty weird . . . Ms.

Yes, that's true.

Anyways, as I was saying, I am going to pull together my own team, become a contractor. I'll even let white bastards like Adam here work for me.

You'll be lucky! said Adam, his head in his arms on the table. Fuck, I'm stoned.

Curly pushed Adam so he half slipped and said, Wake up ya bastard, I'm telling a story to Lucida here. She's interested.

I've heard it all before, said Adam, speaking to the table, having settled back into his position.

So, you see, miss, he said to Lucida, I lost my missus in a car accident a couple of years ago. She was a fine woman, really knowledgeable. An artist.

An artist?

Yes, she sure was.

Lucida couldn't help herself. She was so off her face she felt if she didn't take over Curly's story she would vanish through the floorboards, fall like sheep shit through to the dirt below.

She didn't feel guilty. She felt no despair. But she knew that if she didn't occupy the space of the story immediately her own significance would be diminished and there'd be no return. So she launched into an ars poetica, a justification of her own art that left Curly staring with bemusement. This is ironic, he interrupted on a couple of occasions, adding, I protest that, Lucida, on another. But Lucida let it all hang out, and spoke seamlessly for half-an-hour before Adam lifted his skull from the table and said, I have a story, too!

Adam's Story

HER NOSE OUT of joint, Lucida begrudgingly stopped talking and reached across for the bong, Curly having just packed himself a cone. As Adam started up, she arced up and sucked hard on the bong.

I have no ambition, said Adam, and there's a reason for it. I have found fulfilment already. I know Curly, and his shiny head, and that's enough for me. I came out of the 1980s hate campaigns run by a white supremacist in the Hills outside Perth and I committed unspeakable acts against innocents. But I have been redeemed and I have found purpose out here, on the edge of things.

Shearing fucking sheep, Adam, joked Curly.

Shearing fucking sheep, bro!

Lucida was drifting and sinking at once. She felt like she was going to spew, sucked into the plughole of the southern hemisphere. She wanted to tell them more about herself but when she managed to lift her head to stare into Adam's half closed half open eyes hovering above his hands, she had a memento mori moment that collided her with the particles of Duke's singularity, and she screamed, Duke! Duke! You look hideous!

Adam cocked his eye to the side, then looked filthy. Curly caught it and said, Settle down Adam, I don't like that look . . . it means trouble. Then to Lucida: Never abuse Adam's looks. He can't help it that he's no beauty queen.

Hilarious Bookbinder!

What the fuck? You slut.

You'll never understand, Duke, that you're not the be-all and end-all.

And you've no idea about the dialectic.

Fuck you – either-or either-or ee-or! I'll wipe that smile off your dial.

Come on Adam, leave the lady alone. You'll lose all the respect you've accumulated in your common era life.

Lucida couldn't constrain herself. She climbed with a slovenly style onto the table and tilted at windmills before crashing to the floor, bruising her arm. I bruise quickly, she said, pulling herself up. Time to leave, miss, said Curly, and walk-staggered her back to the hotel where she kissed him goodnight, and said, Sorry, Ben . . . before he closed the door on her and she fell onto the bed and grew rigid with the chill night.

Lucida and the Hermit

DUKE WASN'T *REALLY* a hermit though he had become eremitic towards the end. In those late days on the edge. But Lucida thought of him as a hermit. So when she turned off the bitumen onto a gravel road in search of a secluded place to piss, and saw a tin humpy a few hundred metres into the scrub, she thought, Duke could have lived there. Still studying the humpy from a distance and being conscious of an echidna bristling in the end of a hollowed log, and shuffling her feet to prevent the piss from rolling onto her shoes, she decided she would investigate. She stood up, hitched up her knickers and strained her skirt and pulled a bottle of cleaning gel from her blouse pocket and alcoholised her hands, enjoying the evaporation in the warm air. It was a glorious morning – all sunshine and blue and a bronze-green off the gimlet woodland. Wattles were in bloom and a trail wound its way towards the humpy. She followed it, glancing back at her car, pulling out her keys from her bumbag and pushing click-beep to lock the slightly worse for wear death machine, her damaged Prius. The old codger had done a good job for the three-hundred bucks, but it still looked like it had been out bush bashing.

The humpy's corrugated iron roof flapped a little though there was practically no breeze. It made an eerie sound which excited Lucida. It stimulated her. She was still feeling murky from the skunk weed, but this sharpened her up. In fact, she'd wish she'd asked the fellas for a joint to greet the new day, but she *was* off the stuff, *really*, and didn't want to destroy the equanimity she'd gained post-Duke. A lot of tins, empty food tins – baked beans, spam, and plenty of rusty numbers impossible to identify – were strewn around the outside. There was a cleared area out front with a ring of stones with charcoal and burnt offerings therein. It looked cold, stagnant. A rain tank collected dust and thin deposits of 'dew' from the flapping tin roof. A piece of tattered hessian hung from the doorframe. She pushed it aside.

The hermit was masturbating to a picture of Lucida from a Body as Art spread in *Australian Art*. He said, without breaking concentration on the picture, I knew you would be here before much longer. Just let me finish up and I'll be with you.

Lucida stood in the doorway, the filthy hessian draped over her in a way that would have had The Boys rushing for their cameras, and watched the hermit finish himself off. When he'd done, she said, You'll ruin that spread if you keep depositing that gunk over it. The hermit wiped it off with the back of his hand, tidied himself up, pulling his ragged jeans up without actually getting off the ground, and with an alacrity that Lucida rejoiced in, and said, Come, sit beside me and talk.

The hermit didn't remind Lucida of anyone in particular, let alone Duke, but she said, You are becoming Duke.

I am, said the hermit. Do I inspire you? Can I be your new muse.

'Fraid not, mate, she said, There'll only ever be one Duke.

Seeing the hermit quiver, slightly damaged, she quickly added, But you can be a new character in my theatre of life. The hermit broke into a smile and said, Then all of this has been worthwhile. Now, I will read you some poems I have written in your honour in the Japanese style.

Haiku?

No, the seasons aren't involved. I mean, written in Japanese.

And they were. And the hermit read. And for the second time in two days Lucida was blown away.

*

Lucida had just got back into the Prius when the burning hailstones began to fall from a clear sky. They bounced off the car roof and singed the paint. She saw them pound the humpy and knew the hermit had called them down. He is praying for an apocalypse, she said, And his prayer is being answered. Soon the scrub was on fire and the humpy already melting as she hooked the car around on the dirt road and fishtailed back towards the bitumen. Back on the main road, she looked back at where she'd come from and it was a beautifully clear sky without a wisp of smoke to be seen. She opened the car window and there wasn't a taint of smoke in the air. She closed the window, set the air-conditioning to PERFECT and drove on to the edge of the world itself, to the edge of consumer comfort. Towards Duke and her destiny, out where mining companies ruled the roost and drove all others to oblivion. She pondered how much funding a mining company would be willing to give her if she excused all their activities with a massive art show praising their largesse. Even further than she'd gone before. It was time, she thought, to fully embrace uranium, the ETERNITY of the nuclear cycle. Relatively speaking. She selected a Schumann symphony on the stereo and engaged cruise control and swallowed the bitumen all the way to where it turned to gravel.

*

She'd used a third of a tank reaching the gravel. She would drive until the fuel gauge indicated just above half and then she would turn around and drive back to the last town. A balancing act between fuel and distance she enjoyed. Art is risk.

*

On the edge of the semi-dry salt lake that looked like the lake she had found Duke beside but wasn't, she couldn't help looking for his tin shack. It wasn't there. But not 'of course.' It might have been. But what she did find was a film crew waiting for dusk so they could film desert birds coming in to dabble in the little repositories of fresh water remaining from the last winter rains in the rocky outcrops at its western edge. It was a small crew: camera person, sound person, director and narrator. The narrator was none other than New Ben, but of course Lucida couldn't have known this as he was no longer recognisable to her. He was, after all, NEW. As she pulled over next to their camper van and Hilux ute, New Ben walked over to her car window. She wound it down and he poked his head all the way in and said, We've been expecting you. The star of our show! Other than the parrots, that is.

*

Lucida, for the first time in a long time, felt truly awkward. She turned the screen of her phone into a mirror and checked the scene of her face. Not bad, considering. The scene of the crime, laughed New Ben. I am genuinely confused, said Lucida. Ah, but Duke is as everywhere as the budgies that will come flocking in this evening. Not long to wait now. We've got the primus out and are about to have a cuppa. Join us? Don't worry, it's not an interrogation! I should think not, said Lucida. But I will say that you lot have rather defiled the cathedral of the outback. Like the mining companies, said New Ben, adding, Do you know whose land this really is? Meaning? Who the traditional owners are, Lucida? No idea, but I do know it's going to be *my* land. I am buying the lot of it. I am staking a claim for art's sake. I will set a precedent. Sorry, girl, but art was here a long time before you . . . and, for that matter, Duke! NO! said Lucida. It's not possible. Lucida quivered in the later afternoon and felt suddenly cold. An awareness was blanketing her. Not an epiphany, but something almost as bothering. She thought she heard Duke laughing loud over the lake. A weird, grotesque bird of a laugh full of death. And as distraught as she was, she thanked New Ben. For what? asked New Ben. For releasing me from his grip. Ah, said New Ben, Speaking of which, I've a bone to pick with you. Not now, said Lucida, let's have our tea and go for a walk. Just the two of us. I've got something to share – a gift, a little something special I picked up on a farm a long way south-west of here, a long time ago. It's a revelation. Look out there – a single cloud over the pink lake. It looks like a dragon. It does, said New Ben, who knew what that meant, and who knew his search for justice was almost at an end and that he could only come off second best. Such is life.

The Deposition (against Lucida)

LUCIDA CONSIDERS HERSELF a saviour. She considers herself a full and rounded character. She does not consider herself in an ironic light, not really. She attaches herself to another's biography. It is claimed he was a male. It is claimed Lucida is a female. I am unable to comment on the binary. And I am in no position to say that it wasn't Duke who benefited from Lucida's furthering of his cause, at least in the early days. Duke likely used her as a stepping stone back into corporeality, having long ago become a wraith and a facsimile of the self.

Lucida steps where she shouldn't. She treats taboo like sherbet, and can't get enough of it. She has become a model for young women and non-binary younger people. As such, she has responsibility and she abuses it.

Lucida walks on water. We are told this, but have any of us actually seen it in real life? I mean, I have watched her closely and never seen her walk on water. I've seen her skate on thin ice, but never walk on water.

Lucida quotes Master Sun and says that managing many assets is the same as managing a few, that it's just a matter of divvying it up into parts. This is her excuse for conquest. This is her excuse for marching on over hostile ground. She persists where she is not wanted. And what do we know of her, really?

Lucida is a cipher. I know this. She is based on no one. There are no disclaimers reading: 'All characters herein are fictitious and bear no resemblance to anyone living or read.' None of that, because she is not even a character. She is a lie we attach our desire for story and analogies to. We want to read ourselves or not read ourselves in 'her.' She was born of a font (admittedly, before that font was named or maybe even invented), though a font with many faces. 'Many-coloured glass' scenarios will always be about design, style, and publicity.

Lucida is climate change. Lucida is denial. Lucida is confession. Lucida embraces. All. All the mountains and forests, hills and desert, lakes dry and wet, uranium ponds and slurry pits, slag heaps and stockpiles, are the ground we must negotiate in negotiating her.

Lucida has milked government after government dry whilst shouting her libertarian qualities. Her attributes. When she made billboards out of Freedom Press's edition of Malatesta's *Anarchy*, she (shortly after their success in increasing the Australia-wide sales of electric cars), received a government contract to promote the new Turn Back the Boats anti-refugee policy. Those billboards quoted: 'What is government? The metaphysical tendency*' where * = 'a disease of the mind in which Man, once having by a logical process abstracted an individual's qualities, undergoes a kind of hallucination which makes him accept the abstraction for the real being.'

Lucida claims I tried to give her herpes simplex 2 virus which I did not. I am unaware if she herself has the virus but I do not.

Lucida took a melody I composed on my acoustic guitar sitting on the end of the bed in my hotel room in the Sheraton, Perth, twenty-five years ago and sold it to a rival band.

Lucida's green credentials are based on a manipulation of the data. She is, in fact, a human induced climate change denier par excellence. She feeds data to a senator that makes fact look like fiction to those who want to see the world as such. Subliminal anti-ecological messages are imprinted in all her pro-green artwork.

Lucida never loved Duke. I have with me an early unsigned will of Duke's that shows he wished no individual to benefit from his legacy. I claim that the will Lucida presented was a forgery.

Apostrophes (to Lucida)

She is glorious. She is my inspiration. I am developing an augmented reality game through which her followers 'capture' avatars of Lucida in every place associated with her art, in all places she has been seen and recorded on social media, and on the highest levels, all places she is likely to go that prove to be the case. There's the past, present and future scenarios. She is deliverance. No mere fifteen minutes, she is ETERNITY.

She is glorious. She is my inspiration. I first encountered her playing pool at the Court Hotel. She sauntered in, casual-like, and placed her coins on the side of the table, and held it for hours. We were all riveted. She listened to our stories and told some of her own. She took snaps on her phone and made a collage of us all. She sang a Lady Gaga song with us. She was generous. She was liberated. She promised a future.

She is glorious. She is my inspiration. She is no breeder. She is complete in herself. I did her nails and I have the dust of her filings encased in Perspex. I could offer them on eBay and make a fortune but I am holding on to them. They are displayed in a locked glass cabinet in my shop now. She has such beautiful hands. She could have been a concert pianist. And she dresses down. Casual, chic, expensive with the appearance of everyday wear. That is an art form in itself. She called *me* an 'artiste.'

She is glorious. She is my inspiration. She told me she was having a penis grown in a lab and that she will reveal it to the world when the time is right. She isn't wearing it herself, but letting it live free, a testament to stem cell research and art. She is a pioneer. She is not stuck on the body but releasing it. She is whizziwig. What you see is what you get.

She is glorious. She is my inspiration. She travelled in West Africa during the Ebola crisis and was without fear. She encouraged people to touch her. She had such beautiful images taken of these moments. She glowed. There are witnesses. She travelled south and refused blood diamonds. She was offered so many diamonds. She only took the pure offerings.

She is glorious. She is my inspiration. When I saw her appear, I knew she was the answer. Trapped in an isolated city, wordless, I saw her walking along the river, speaking with the black swans, and I knew I had found my purposes. She began as a groupie, and so did I. She made her own music and I make mine. I've had my photo taken with the rest of the band in my parents' big bathtub while they are overseas. I am covered in suds, naked beneath. I am one with my band. We hypnotise our audiences. We think of Lucida as we play. We collect seashells on the seashore. We spike the drinks of enemies and they never suspect.

She is glorious. She is my inspiration. I too have metaphorically killed my parents. I tell the truth I want to tell. I reinvent them and myself. The beasts. I never hit them, they hit me. They don't hit but they do metaphorically. I am free. I am tuned into my cohort and won't be a slave to their reputations. I am the centre of Lucida's attention because a lot of her is me and vice versa. I find love and support in the mental health community who know how to untwist my story to fit with the truth they've provided. I love them for this. I love Lucida's struggle with the authorities and their coming on side. I reject the diagnosis. I am the queen of all she surveys, I am the Duke of Wellington. I am whatever I want her to want me to be. I have exquisite hair. I am multitalented. I am an actor. I would have been a television star if it weren't for my parents. Lucida has shown me the way. She is my model. She risks all. She is ageless. She is in tune with my generation. She calls us Generation Absolute. We don't need the system. We are the system. All those clichés foisted on us by my parents. I am the hand that feeds me. I, Lucida, and me. Duke is irrelevant. We who know her know that. She made him and now she forgets him and he vaporises.

She is glorious. She is my inspiration. I like her again and again. I loveheart everything she does. I am hands on and hands free. Lucida makes clouds. She offers us planets to colonise when this one wears out. The security agencies of the world listen in to the chatter around her by way of relief. She will deliver the enemies. She is just and she is justice.

She is glorious. She is my inspiration. I took the bullet for her. When the assassin dressed in mufti stepped out of the subway in Sydney I saw him with his akubra beard and I ran between him and Lucida who was shopping for herself in the retail stories of tomorrow, and I took the bullet. I didn't draw it to her attention, it wouldn't have been becoming. I think she was with the ex-Speaker of the House. That hairdo, just the kind of personal accessory Lucida would enjoy. But neither of them noticed. And I took those invisible bullets in my heart, and swelled up with joy. The assassin blended back into the body of voters, and Lucida emerged from a shop wearing an *I am Not Racist, I am Australian* t-shirt. She thinks of us all. She is without prejudice. She will dine at Kirribilli House one night, and in a shelter for the homeless the next. She markets us to the future. She is gloss and matte. She is all conjunctions. She is glorious. She is my inspiration.

She is glorious. She is my inspiration. I didn't know I was in despair. I wasn't aware. Then she filled me with despair. She made me feel I'd done things I'd been sure I hadn't done. I knew my guilt where there was no evidence. She made me feel bad about myself without foundation and I am eternally grateful for that.

Awareness. And then, aware of my eternal existence, I despaired more and *knew* that I existed. I found purpose checking the Perth water supply for methamphetamine usage. Thirty-five kilos a day revelation. I sampled the sewers and came up Trumps. Despair has more uses than happiness. When I go, when I select my moment, it will be to drown in the slough of the city, to drown in its rapid transit sewage. That is civilisation, the accumulation of vast amounts of waste fast and localised. All joining up. The superhighway of waste. I am filth. I am aware. I am ETERNAL like Lucida. She is glorious. She is my inspiration.

Lucida Shucks Duke Off Like a Husk: A Retrospective (or, A Time Slip)

LUCIDA SORTED THROUGH her papers for the university archive. A fire sale. She had a manila folder with some of her primary school stories and poems, and a few scribbles she thought more of than her teachers. I will replicate these as wallpaper. They are free indirect discourse. There was one story in particular that tickled her fancy. It was written in grade three in half-printing half-running writing style. A transitional piece in more ways than one, she told herself. She gathered The Boys together, who appeared in her massive warehouse apartment with its gigantic canvases against the heavy jarrah support beams as soon as she called them, as she required an audience. The Boys were in the studio adjoining the main room where Lucida open-planned her existence. In the studio that had been working on her next gigantic canvas: photos of her recent journey to London transposed and then painted out in florescent colours. Her particular focus on that visit was Greenwich, especially the building in which the nuclear reactor Jason had been housed. Her paintings were full of radium.

Boys! she said, and they scurried to sit at her feet, Boys, a reading. And so, standing before the semi-circle of her horrible workers, she read:

Little Red Riding Hood

The forest has been chopped down so I, Little

179

*Red Riding Hood, can't find Grandma's House.
It was in the forest but there is no forest now.
There are lots of stumps and some men with bull-
dozers, but there's no forest and no Grandma.
She must be hungry. I will find another forest.
I have found one with a big tree in the middle with a twirling ladder that goes almost up
to the clouds. There's a hut on top of the tree.
Grandma must live there. I will climb the tree
and look out over the forest. I see a big dog.
It could be an Alsatian and they are scary. It
asks me where I am going. To Grandma's. She's
hungry. He says, Look, if you take that path
you'll get there quicker. I take the path, climb
the tree, and reach the hatch into Grandma's
sky hut. Grandma is in her little bed. She says,
Dearie, I am famished. Come here so I can see
you and all that grub in your bag. But I feel
odd and say, What a big nose you have. All
the better to smell the good grub with. What
big eyes you have. All the better to take a good
look at you, my little plum. What big teeth you
have. All the better to eat you with. But then
the Alsatian leaps out of bed and falls through
the hatch which I left open which isn't very
smart for a dog smart enough to climb a tree.
Good riddance I say and sit down and eat the
grub. Then I hear an angry noise and I look
down through the hatch and some guys are
chainsawing the tree down. Then I wake.*

The Boys cheered. Now, said Lucida, If that's not prophetic, prescient, and the rest of it, I don't know what is. And, she said, it's lusciously and perversely sexual as well, as any Little Red Riding version should be. And the beauty is, I didn't know it at the time. Innocence is a grand thing for exploitation. It's all encoded, these cautionary bits and pieces. It's a riot. I want it spread far and wide. I want to copyright whatever can be copyrighted. Get on to it boys!

*

But the truth be had, Lucida was feeling flat. The wind was no longer in her sails. She lacked purpose. Post-Duke (now a husk), she found little to desire or admire. She had started frequenting a small, private club in a light industrial suburb near the hills, and dallied with applying nipple clamps and having nipple clamps applied to herself, but it was, in the end, only shallow, hollow fun. The best bit was wearing masks. She revelled in pretend anonymity – all knew who she was but pretended not to. Her safety word was, Climax, which confused things just enough. The madam was an old school friend who'd seized her opportunity with the mining boom and had gone from being a speech therapist to working girl to madam in a very short period of time. She lived in a limestone house now with a wine cellar and many pieces of Duke's and Lucida's artworks in her many bedrooms and corridors. She indulged Lucida. But Lucida was bored and empty and withering away inside.

On a whim, Lucida rang Old Ben who had died and been resurrected. He said, Lucida! I'll be there in two days (he was in Tokyo, after a stint trying to clean up Fukushima reactor one, a process which made the words 'slow' and 'gradual' redundant). And he was.

Lucida and (Old) Ben. Ben her love her life her purpose for being. Duke was a mere shadow, a puppet on the edge of her life's stage. Lucida met Ben at the airport personally, bought a few hometown souvenirs while waiting for him to get through customs, then whisked him away to her warehouse. Lucida had arranged for the caterer to leave shortly after their arrival, meal on the table. She didn't do any introductions.

Amazing place you have here, Lucida.

Yes, I bought it off a mining magnate's son. It was his city playpen – their compound is in the country, set in lush rolling hills with Arabians. Horses, that is.

Yes, guessed that. I am proud of you, Lucida, you've come from nothing to everything.

I would never say it was nothing. But I am known for my false modesty.

A shiny car and shiny life, Lucida!

Now you're being sarcastic, Ben. That's not nice. Lucida crossed and uncrossed her legs under the table. It was a long table and they were at opposite ends which didn't really work as the dishes were at Lucida's end and Ben had to keep getting up. Lucida had catered vegan for the night just to make Ben happy. Or rather, so Ben would actually stay. He had no flexibility and this annoyed but enticed her as well.

You see, Lucida, I just don't get it. I get the drugs. I get the sex. I get the art. But I don't get the gloss. What are you actually doing with your life.

Being a success, darling. It's better that way. And it didn't take you much to rush back from your serious activities, did it.

No, it didn't. But I resent what you did to me, Lucida.

We will take a stroll along the river after dinner. It is a balmy night. Swallows will be darting about. There's a band playing at the local pub I think you'd like. Some of your old friends still playing.

Oh? Who?

Pulse.

Fuck! They're still around. Pub band thirty years ago and pub band now. I don't know if I could stand it.

Don't be a stick in the mud, Ben. I need zest, I need renewal. You'll help me with this.

Always your servant, Lucida. I guess you're going to take that call.

I shouldn't, should I. But she did. She took the smart phone from her pocket, told the caller to WAIT, and levered her way from the table and walked to the far end of the warehouse and into the studio to take it. Ben, whose point of view becomes paramount at this moment, leans back in his chair, tilts his head back, and stares at the roof beams. What the fuck am I doing here? Then he hears Lucida scream, and turning sharply he knocks the chair back and staggers and falls to the ground. She is running towards him, yelling, Ben! Ben! You will be the death of me. You must leave leave leave!

And Ben left and flew back to Tokyo two days later. And Lucida started work on her Mary Godwin and Percy Shelley on Mary Wollstonecraft's grave series, which thrust her into the stratosphere yet again.

Lucida Rewrites the Last Days of Duke

LUCIDA: IT WAS a cold wind that blew that hot day. And he was alive in the morning, and dead in the evening. His body was likely eaten by the wild dogs, his skeleton bleached by the moonlight and powdered by nuclear sun of the following morning attacking through the perforated ozone layer and blown away over the dry lake by the powerful wind that picked up from the south and blew hot and furious. I left there burnt, my skin bubbling and falling off me. I left there in my hire car, a Jeep Renegade.

Duke: I had become inspired by my own nakedness. By the world my body had to offer on the edge of the lake. The glare, the snowburn reflection off the gypsum, salts. I had given up the flesh. The large-breasted lovers I sucked on to feed me my infancy. I had paid off my assistant and told her I could not fill her maternity bras. She called me a misogynist and I agreed this was likely. So I renounced my position in the world. I no longer haunted the streets of world cities writing on blank walls with clay paint that could be washed off, I no longer claimed my ephemerality as central. It was time for me to go outside the news, to experience events as they happened and not to try to influence them for good or bad. I remember walking with my crew, all of us dressed like boys from an American hood, reverse baseball caps and Nike shoes, a sack of spray cans, and all the middle-class walls of Copenhagen going down to our American English like ninepins. We painted Glocks on the walls of the

Lutheran churches and peace signs on military barracks.

Lucida: Your nakedness was nothing to crow about, Duke. Pitiful specimen of a man. And always going on about your own suffering. You middle-class wanker. Your European sensibilities, your recolonising Centralia. You speak English with hooks, though you claim you can't remember a word of Danish.

Duke: You took me by surprise, saying you'd pierced your clitoral hood with a rivet gun. I mean, I had to look to see you were lying. But I looked. And then you had me, Lucida.

Lucida: Had what? You? Don't make me laugh.

Duke: You think you can free yourself of the dust by denigrating me?

Lucida: Absolutely.

Duke: When I was seven I was taken to Perth to visit my maternal grandmother who cleaned movie theatres. She collected Jaffas that had been thrown from the lounge into the stalls and preserved them in aspic in large jars which she displayed in her small living room. She believed she had talked to Christ, and I believe she had. I stayed with her for a month and went with her in the early hours to help clean the theatres. It was a working holiday. I stayed on Copenhagen time and avoided jetlag. I had a Kodak Instamatic she gave me. She said there are 24 photos to be taken on this roll and I can only afford to have one roll developed, so use them wisely. I had a single flash cube so could take four night shots. I took those in the theatre; I also photographed King's park War Memorial, the Narrows Bridge leaning over the rail on the southside, the cement works at Rivervale, and the rest of my grandmother who dressed up in various costumes she'd collected from op shops over the years. In one, she was Lawrence of Arabia. I slept in her bed in a room with heavy drapes drawn against a sun so fierce I thought I would die. We slept on a sheet

on the bed, naked. We embraced our isolation and aloneness and
I renounced all that I had been. An old man visited every couple
of days and went into the room alone with grandmother and
they made cat and dog sounds. I sat outside her bedroom door
crying. How would I survive being sent home to Copenhagen.
Within a month I spoke Australian.

Lucida: I went looking for your family on Strøget and there
was no trace of them. I don't believe you've ever even visited
Denmark.

Duke: Just around the corner from Rådhuspladsen, off the
Vesterbrogade, is an adult shop that's been there for decades. Part
of the Scandinavian sexual revolution. When I was twelve I went
in there, unhindered and unquestioned, and flipped through
magazines of bestiality and coprophilia and other fetish practices.
The photography and printing were of an exceptionally high
standard. I fixated on the faces of the participants, animal and
human, and felt their loss, their isolation, then hopelessness. I
wanted to paint that. I wanted to know how to paint the misery.

Lucida: You're a liar. You never were an artist. You're a nothing.
A self-obsessed nothing.

Duke: There seems little action where there is bleach but there
is so much. It changes everything. Grandmother's hands were
stained by bleach. Down to her bones.

Lucida: When No Rush in the Gold Rush dropped by with
his gadget to find uranium and whatever else he told you that
whatever he found out there would be good as gold.

Duke: Water runs deep but they'll eventually reach it.

Lucida: I went with him, Duke. I went with him under the cover
of night when the dark sky pricked us with starlight. We were
saturated. You are impotent. That's the truth.

Duke: Once I was pushed into a urinal and the boys pissed on me. I looked up as the first arc of piss left its eye and gushed down into my eyes. But I saw the beauty of departure, the beauty of allegory, in my suffering. *Damnosa hereditas*, and all is ETERNITY.

Lucida: That's the first useful thing you've said and I bet you twisted it from somewhere else. Another source.

Duke:　Who lokede on that park withoute,
　　　　Portrayed on the wal but doute
　　　　Are alle develes and depe helle,
　　　　Ful feendliche on to see and felle . . .

Lucida: Pathetic.

*

The art of the interview is in either making the interviewee overly comfortable or making them anxious. Either way, they'll say something they regret. When I asked Duke what his great secret was, he came right out and told me, adding, Don't put that in the interview. Don't tell anyone. I mean, really, a red rag to a bull or what? He believed that if I revealed the location of the bird the gawkers and exploiters would come, but what he didn't realise was that they were there already. In *me* reside the numerical masses. I am entire of myself. I have a duty of care to my followers. I don't mind taking the rap for that, in fact I am proud. I mean, seriously, I drove into one of those birds on the way up, not far from Duke's shack. It was hopping flapping sort of flying across the road at dusk, so what do you expect. I am not saying I wanted to hit it, but there you go. And there were dingoes out there as well. They were always snuffling around the place, Duke said. He liked them. I like their silence when they come here, he said. I paint their tracks – I am a fossicker of sorts, he said. Adding it like wisdom or a horror story, depending on your sensibilities.

I saw the Devil pass through the tin wall, he said, when I asked about his red phase. That was long before the Devil – the red phase, that is – but it still lingers. They were the kind of answers he gave. It could be exasperating. But then I began to think, there's method here. He is allowing me to interview him after all. Bit like those artists or actors who say, I don't know *how* all this happened to little ol' me. Or: getting a critic friend to write: s/he is not a self-promoter but their new book is a stunner. Or: the academic critic who calls the interviewer like me – as I was – an opportunist when s/he has gone through promotion after promotion through presenting self-praising self-critiques to assessment boards. You see a lot of that in the industry, even at the grunge end I inhabited.

I hitched a lift once when I was starting out. I hitched a lift all the way to another salt lake way out past Menzies to see these human figures doing their primeval parody. And the artist spat as he spoke and loomed close and I thought, Chthonic. That could so easily be me, spitting and appropriating and getting the necessary permissions to do so by trick or treat. I can be as patronising as the rest. I can be a white rapper who claims black authority. I can be an inverter of racism. I can tie them all in knots. I wouldn't say this to anyone but you, but the time has come, New Ben, to bring someone new into my circle – my gift to you! And here we are, an hour's walk from camp and your little police helpers doing their film crew thing and way too far away to hear your calls for help. And if the wind which blows against you, should falter and they hear something in the dim distance, they will shake with fear under their bluster and hustle the camera and the sound to capture a rare feat of nature. You silly fucker. As if I wasn't on to you from the beginning. You're a carnivore and you'll die a carnivore intruder's death. You're a predator that's been predated on. It's a horrible death, I believe. Are you waiting for the guys in the old Holden that's kept alive by bush mechanics who ply these sandy tracks where the goannas swish their tails to come to your rescue? Water? I am grateful you have *plenty*. I never come prepared. Just enough fuel to get me back to a session of skunk weed and a couple of lovely fellas

I'll let fuck me senseless if they want. But they won't. They've other things to think about. Have you ever thought about who walks this way, this ETERNITY. What stories are real stories, are a young fella's or a young girl's heritage that your type fuck up? I mock you all. And you, in your older manifestation, so ready to join a protest, so ready to get hyped up and when that cause is lost to move on to the next. Jeez, make a stand New Ben. Okay, I'll tell you. Yes, yes I did unto him what I will do unto you. But it can't hurt me, it can only make me stronger, as I am born again. But I say it to the wind, to the heat, as I burn to a cinder, because I detest ambiguity, I detest loose threads and dead ends. I ask God for forgiveness. I take responsibility. I have, thanks to you all, grown. And that, surely, is what it's all about, bro. And 'murder' is just a word in a dictionary, in film scripts, on lengths of wallpaper.

Lucida Syndrome

IN THE 2030s this was a byword for the delusions suffered by the over-famous. In the 2010s television reality stars, overhyped pop stars, and politicians, were already suffering from the condition, as had been the case since Achilles got the rap he'd got from some blind poet seer, raving up the case of Greek monoculturalism and conquest, but by the 2020s, when Lucida occupied the mental and emotional landscapes of a world stripped back to the bare bones, drowning and choking on its own goo and afflatus, and most in The West were famous in their own minds if they lived beyond the age of ten, it was a fait accompli.

Later, when she was cleansing herself of her past, Lucida claimed she had suffered from Stockholm Syndrome when spending time with Duke out in the shack in Centralia, and that her accomplishments were all the more amazing and unique given this. His silence bullied me into overinflating his memory. I identified with my captor because I felt I'd gone to him of my own free will but I realise now that he'd projected his will through the media and lured me to my demise. In his passing I became the servant of his memory.

Further, Lucida claimed to suffer Stendhal Syndrome every time she beheld her own artworks, and that overwhelmed and swooning, she was often left so incapacitated by her own suffusions and effusions of beauty and brute reality, that she had to step out of the room and hand over to The Boys. A celebrity doctor analysed her condition on television and noted that though it was dangerous to Lucida it was of great benefit to humanity. Further, he added, it created new lines of definition between East and West and that in an age of the boundaries blurring, this was helpful to the privileged who felt under siege. There is something sublimely self-sacrificing in Lucida's messianic behaviour, he noted, but if she doesn't watch her diet and exercise regularly, we will all feel it. We must get behind her in life. Fox News fell into line early on and had an hour-long programme every day at primetime on the 'State of Lucida,' to bring comfort to the gun owners of America even though Lucida had been known to mock gun owners in her collages. It's a matter of interpretation, her NRA supporters insisted. Her saying NO to guns is a wake-up call to gunowners to speak out and say YES. That's the nature of art – we understand Lucida who understands most artists don't understand.

*

Early on, Lucida handed social media activities – in the main – over to The Boys. She occasionally tweeted and uploaded a selfie, occasionally used Instagram, Facebong, Wham and ThanX, but things changed so fast she didn't have the time to keep up. If I am not making the changes, she said, it is up to others to follow those (other) changes. But she inevitably changed the activities and patterns of all social media The Boys used on her behalf. Throwback Thursdays quickly became a finding or manufacturing of images from Lucida's past, her monumental moments. Find a Lucida image and post. Most images were of young people dressed up as Lucida (say, as the Minotaur, prancing around her bone-strewn labyrinth and shitting daintily here and there), but some were shots from Lucida's actual past. These, if seen by Lucida, inevitably brought legal action and a punitive arm of The Boys was established to track down the posters and 'sort them.' This is likely when Old Ben *really* became New Ben[7] – having posted a Goth image of Lucida sculling Tequila – he was found and pushed around and the original Polaroid 'removed' from him and threats issued and so forth. But it's digitalised now, he insisted with a mouth full of blood. Lucida is interested in hard copies. There are no hard copies she doesn't have herself. If it'd had a negative, you'd be dead, man. And Ben, his brains rattling around his sconce, changed in decisive and irresolvable ways. His chrysalis

7 See *The Oxford American Dictionary*, re 'catharsis.'

had burst and his love of Lucida turned to a pathological hatred. Lucida who could see all, didn't perceive the depth of Ben's resentment. Thus his rearranged face meant he could not look prettily on her any more. So when he downloaded Lucida, the Absolute Phone App, it was not to upload possible generative pasts of Lucida, to filter with 'Slumberoo' and 'Volcano,' but to show himself other than what he was – to be 'out there' and to feel on top of it, but to disguise his real mood, his real intention. He no longer went out in desultory ways with people who reminded him of Lucida, he no longer sought out those with Granny Hair silver at nightclubs, but sought out the few haters and detesters of art, who grew large formless and wild gardens in The Hills, and who deplored wind chimes and home-fired pottery.

*

In the Age of Lucida everyone was becoming artist and becoming not an artist as there could only be one Artist, in truth, and that was Lucida. Lucida Syndrome was not an accusation of Lucida, because she was Fame personified – she made no *effort* because all fame had become hers – but rather a comment on those who in becoming famous overwhelmed themselves. Lost in the filters of capitalism, the self became a self unrecognisable and as such *art.* In the absolute nature of self, 'free will' necessarily meant the loss of that old-fashioned control mechanism 'identity.' Lose identity and be liberated. Find self and be entire in yourself. Lucida spoke of capitalism as a naughty child that was fun and bothersome, creative and damaging, but to be nurtured and trained towards the individual's need. The numerical masses, she said, consume to keep the self afloat. She looked rapturous when she said these things for The Boys to record. The online Left glorified her. Hackers left her sites alone as they were the very essence of their antisocial lust for attention. She understood them all.

*

It was asked, by some, New Ben included, who precisely *were* The

Boys? Well . . . thereby hangs a tale. Of course, they weren't actually (in truth) always male. And of course, most weren't 'artists' by
trade. Few had formal training. Some were recruited from outlaw
motorcycle gangs, some from the fashion industry, some had done
signwriting apprenticeships (these were the real artists), and many
from IT backgrounds. Their numbers hovered around a dozen, but
at times there were more or less. Though Lucida was their supreme
leader, they generally operated amongst themselves by consensus.
None was above the other. The ex-ASIO agent tried to assume control, but he never really succeeded. Most of the other Boys assumed
he was Lucida's inside man, but they could never be sure. He never
missed a meeting, an opening, or major event. Some conjectured he
was a double agent, still in the service of the Australian government
and keeping an eye on Lucida and benefiting from the de-facto
diplomatic immunity that seemed to extend to all Lucida's entourage when globetrotting. But he made valuable utilitarian input
into the team – it was his idea (acknowledged publicly as Lucida's,
of course) to stage the campaign: *Confront your demons: show your
carbon footprint to the world through travel.*

The Boys, when in Sydney, Melbourne, Adelaide, or Perth,
shared digs. A small apartment building was bought in each city
close to Lucida's home and studio. When travelling, the entourage
occupied the top floor of certain hotels, orbiting around Lucida.
This was in the 'settled years' – earlier, they came from wherever to
be near her. Lucida's agent saw that it gelled, and Lucida's lawyers
saw that it was locked into place. The Boys, once in, never left by
choice though were shed (and often vanished) at varying intervals.
New members of the studio were inducted with rituals never spoken
of even by those who had survived leaving, who walked around in a
daze with a haunted, stricken look on their surgically altered faces.

It was not unusual for one of The Boys to develop a crush on
Lucida. She swanned into a room and made them float. But there
was no transitioning into a favoured position – she might sleep
with you if she felt so inclined, but it would never go further. Sex
for Lucida was, for a time, a performative act, so if you were chosen,
inevitably the cameras would follow. Performance anxiety didn't just
equate with maleness. The series of home porn scenarios shot in this

way became know as the Deification Series and were streamed live but later converted to home theatre holographics with interactive versions. The faces of The Boys who participated were erased and only their bodies shown in hyperreal taste-touch-test mode. Lucida said that it was an act against body shaming. You can't shame if you don't have a face. Too much of our culture is about facial recognition. The torso sculpture – headless and bottomless – was back with a vengeance.

*

New Ben thought, at first, he could bring Lucida down via The Boys. Cracking their code. Infiltrating with one of his agents. But that was not possible. Ex-ASIO's tentacles reached far and without exposing himself, but sacrificing one of his own agents, Ben discovered that impostors wouldn't even get past first base of the selection process. Further, if there was a whiff about them, they simply vanished and no amount of surveillance or scrutiny would reveal their whereabouts, never mind what had come to pass. It was if they were erased from all existence. Ben had to think long-term and tangentially. He had to rediscover Lucida and stop basing his assumptions and actions on the old Lucida, the Lucida he had adored and worshipped. He still had a small makeup pot that held, tightly compressed, Lucida's pubic hairs, which he gathered together carefully after she shaved herself because she knew that the lead guitarist of the old stadium rock band liked his girls that way. I want that interview, she'd told Old Ben, who felt like all life was being crushed out of him. And seeing his hangdog look, she said, I own my passivity. I own how I will turn it. If I want to be a member of the Communist Party, if I want you to collect mistresses for me, if I want to own this city as if it's 1945 and the war has just ended, then I will. This is my liberation. It's not an illness and I am feeding no one but myself. This decrepit rock star with his dangerous little lusts is on the way out and I am going to help hasten the journey. In the end, he will ask for *my* pardon. Same old tricks, same old dog. Ben looked on in wonderment, and reached to touch the itchy, bothered skin, but Lucida slapped his hand away and said, *Look*, darl, don't touch!

Øieblikket

TAKING A MEGAPHONE to the world, Lucida was having no more of the homunculus Duke distracting her from her direct communication with her deified self. She woke up to the fact that she'd been in denial, and went down to the river to bathe. That the river was dry and blooming with red algal dust in its self-concept, and that the fisheries department was trying to stock this very same dust with prawns hatched in tanks, was only mildly distracting. She called on all those souls who had blocked her path to herself. She especially damned the Bens – Old and New. She tore at her skin, she broke into her womb, and tore out the death that had resided for so long inside her. The land is my hospital, she said, as The Boys rushed to patch her up, to weld her back together. But she was having none of it. I am my own punishment, she said, as they conveyed her message to the legions who lay in wait, ready to burst up out of their networked boxes and into the smudged atmosphere.

Lucida Postscript: Mirror Mirror on the Wall

QUEEN

MIRROR, MIRROR on the wall
Who in the land is fairest of all?

Mirror

You, O Queen,
you are the fairest of all.

Queen

As you can never lie,
I know you tell the truth.
But I will ask again
when time has passed,
as time has its own reality.

Mirror, mirror on the wall
Who in the land is fairest of all?

Mirror

Yours is a sublime beauty, O Queen,
but I must declare Snow White
a beauty beyond compare.

Queen

As you can never lie,
I know you tell the truth,
which fills me full of wrath
and makes me hate that girl –

the mere sight of her
makes me sick to the core.
I will have no rest,
day or night, while she exists.

I will call a huntsman –
take Snow White
deep into the forest,
cut out her heart

and bring it to me
on a plate.

*

A sheep's heart buried in the back yard, in the black coastal sand, quickly became blown. The maggots were picked out and placed in pollard and taken in containers down to Coogee Beach jetty where they looked out towards Garden Island, a short distance from the meatworks and power station and found themselves skewered on small hooks and dangled in the lipid-green water to lure garfish to their doom. That was in the early 1970s. And now my heart is buried and blown, and will be used as bait. I am old now but as we live under our skins of sunblock and our bodies have transmuted with the accumulation of nanoparticles I am no less glamorous, no less in demand. My giant paintings are as big as skyscrapers now, and in fact three of the forty skyscrapers of Perth alone show my artworks at night. During the day, they are thin veils that glimmer in the red-gold of the poisonous sun. I am bigger than Louise Bourgeois ever was. I am the spider at the centre of global warming. I am a libertarian goddess smoking bongs full of hydro and tobacco. I am the mirror to my own accomplishment. I will see humanity out.

But I have buried my heart and will let it be blown. Those I have loved are long gone, and they never even knew I loved them. I still listen to Zeppelin's 'Ramble On' when I shower. I still watch *Sid and Nancy* on a regular basis, and have switched formats of viewing as formats have changed over time. I have donated vast amounts of money to good causes. I have been sponsored by major mining companies and have watched them bury themselves. I have three chairs of fine arts named after me around the world. I have built seawalls and divided seas themselves. I have seen agriculture move under vast glass domes. I have had myself cloned, though the results were less appealing to me than to others. But I am *giving* in that way.

I recall an occasion I want recounted at my funeral. It was with (Old) Ben. We were eating in a food court in Perth after a gig. The court usually closed at eight but on Friday nights it was open late. It was a boring gig and we hung around the green room hoping to score something, anything, when a bouncer came out, pissed, and bashed Ben. He was bleeding and shit and I led him out holding his nose and said, You won't be snorting speed tonight, babe (I said babe at that time), and he broke out laughing spraying blood all over the show. Anyway, after I'd cleaned him up in a public toilet where the usual stuff was going on, we went to have a meal and every time he chewed he yelped. So this big bikie bastard comes over to the table with his patch glowing on his jacket, and he says to us, Youse guys seen some trouble tonight. Yes, we says, A bouncer at the XXX concert got a bit rough. Fucker, said the bikie. I like the look of youse kids. Want some action? Yeah, we said, though Ben's face was all warped and twisted. So we chew our last chews and follow the bastard out into the dark alleyway alongside the food court, and he pulls out a baggie of crystals and shakes them in the half-light so they glimmer like a supernova. Angel Dust, kids, he says. Make you think you're as strong as an ox. I reckon if you have a blast of this and head back down to the venue that bouncer or someone else connected to the concert will still be there and you can take your revenge. We loved the sound of this. Ben wasn't so noble back then, though he was the first to sugar a bulldozer's tank and didn't mind a punch-up with the Nazi punks down Freo way. We didn't have any picks on us, but the bikie took us down to an adult shop and through the greasy curtains and out the back where his missus was giving one-on-one strips and headjobs, and he said to a shocked customer, don't worry about us, as we passed through into a back room at the back of the back room, where there was a minuscule bathroom. The bikie got a glass of water and a spoon and produced a couple of needles that looked blunt and none too clean which is probably where my hep before it was eliminated sourced from and we tasted the pure high of that glorious stoner laugh serious film in a worried America of the time, *Angel Dusted,* which is so ludicrous today now we've seen them eliminate themselves as a nation by turning their weapons simultaneously against themselves, discovering that the Mason-Dixie line means fuck all when you start shooting off nuclear weapons at each other . . . and we went down to the venue at high speed, a few blocks away, the bikie coming along for the ride – his name was Ralph – and there were just cleaners around and we asked where the crew had gone and they said drinking down at the City Hotel which stays open late late late and sure enough there they all were and our bouncer and we dragged him out into the street and Angel Dusted him and I felt the beauty of display, of performance, of not judging a bikie by his jacket, his patch.

I keep '28' parrots in a glass aviary in my glass penthouse on the top of the tallest Perth skyscraper. I prefer Perth, now so many other cities have fallen. The fat cats of Perth are dirigibles around my beacon. They hang around for the scraps. Swollen

seas and yet, no river. I worked that one: art and science. Just
one culture now, the Culture of Lucida. I am totem to all. Yes, I
keep '28' parrots, the only non-cloned colony in existence. I love
the red above their beaks. Their splendid yellow bellies. I have
plenty of non-GM grain brought in for them to snack on. They
are my inspiration these days. I look back to nature.

I had a *child*. Late. I was in my early sixties. Perfectly possible.
Duke's child. Not the homunculus, now dust with the dried red
algae in the river that once was, but a come-again, living child.
A born child. A child that left my body. He'd had sperm frozen
as part of a show and I bought the artwork. Cost me millions.
The little beast that issued forth during the Caesarean was clearly
not Duke's. Duke hoodwinked us to the end. I doubt he had
any potent sperm to tap. Anyway, enough of him. And the baby,
which got farmed out for medical research. I was considered a
model mother for allowing he that was more of me than me, to
be used for the common commercial good.

Now that there is no industry no poverty no food no entertainment no war and only art, I feel I can lay claim to mortal
deity status. I am proud to be one of the Five Living Deities.
All who starve to death, those last jarrah trees that fall, that last
stretch of coast to no longer be coast, those tortured and stripped
back to component parts are Art. They are ART and ETERNAL.
And the final typeface, they say, as the written word is being
phased out, will be, by terra and lunar and Martian agreement,
Lucida Deity. I am so honoured. I am the printing press of their
desires. I am the embodiment of their dreams. I am the law. I am
the entity before which they tremble. I am their sex. Duke said,
I am a response to my own ignorance. I answer myself. A typical
non-answer when I asked him what excited him beyond art.
What his favourite food was. His favourite colour. He rambled,
you know, or was silent. A long floating ghostly silence which
creeped me out. He was a stupid, bumbling fool. He'd ask me
how best to paint a crow, how best to show nothingness on canvas, how best to make a spiral that wasn't a spiral. His ridiculous
features. His ridiculous paunchy gut. And he was skinny with
it. And then he'd burst out with: I am simply a *Hegelian fool!* I

knew the echo, I knew he was performing. I had my researchers on the case night and day in later years, and I can prove he was closer to the school dunce than the school maverick. He marbled paper and made book bindings, he painted a horse drinking at a trough, and sang in the *Anglican* church choir. A small Church it was. He was never a Lutheran to stop being a Lutheran. He was no longer a Lutheran because he'd never been a Lutheran. In a clear sky he was a cloud of his own imagining. I hear the cock of eternity crowing and I can't be bothered to rise up out of bed. The Boys are long dead and there is no one to shake the sleep out of my blanket. The desert is deadly cold at night. The spirits close in as the fire vanishes. They refuse my demands they leave. They refuse to be called art. It's so trivial, this end. So without style. So bland. So fated. I will read Aristophanes's *The Clouds* to my parrots. They are slowly learning to speak Lucida. I will be gentle with them and start at the beginning:

ὦ Ζεῦ βασιλεῦ τὸ χρῆμα τῶν νυκτῶν ὅσον:
ἀπέραντον. οὐδέποθ᾽ ἡμέρα γενήσεται;
καὶ μὴν πάλαι γ᾽ ἀλεκτρυόνος ἤκουσ᾽ ἐγώ:
οἱ δ᾽ οἰκέται ῥέγκουσιν: ἀλλ᾽ οὐκ ἂν πρὸ τοῦ.
ἀπόλοιο δῆτ᾽ ὦ πόλεμε πολλῶν οὕνεκα,
ὅτ᾽ οὐδὲ κολάσ᾽ ἔξεστί μοι τοὺς οἰκέτας.
ἀλλ᾽ οὐδ᾽ ὁ χρηστὸς οὑτοσὶ νεανίας
ἐγείρεται τῆς νυκτός, ἀλλὰ πέρδεται
ἐν πέντε σισύραις ἐγκεκορδυλημένος.
ἀλλ᾽ εἰ δοκεῖ ῥέγκωμεν ἐγκεκαλυμμένοι.
ἀλλ᾽ οὐ δύναμαι δείλαιος εὕδειν δακνόμενος
ὑπὸ τῆς δαπάνης καὶ τῆς φάτνης καὶ τῶν χρεῶν
διὰ τουτονὶ τὸν υἱόν. ὁ δὲ κόμην ἔχων
ἱππάζεταί τε καὶ ξυνωρικεύεται
ὀνειροπολεῖ θ᾽ ἵππους: ἐγὼ δ᾽ ἀπόλλυμαι
ὁρῶν ἄγουσαν τὴν σελήνην εἰκάδας:
οἱ γὰρ τόκοι χωροῦσιν. ἅπτε παῖ λύχνον,
κἄκφερε τὸ γραμματεῖον, ἵν᾽ ἀναγνῶ λαβὼν
ὁπόσοις ὀφείλω καὶ λογίσωμαι τοὺς τόκους.

Selected Dalkey Archive Paperbacks